Joe K
True Ghost Stories

Real-Life Encounters!

**Volume
Ghost Stories from
TEXAS!**

More Than 150 Recent Encounters
From the Lone Star State!

I

Joe Kwon's True Ghost Stories

VOLUME 3
Ghost Stories from
Texas

Joe Kwon, Inc.

Joe Kwon's True Ghost Stories. Copyright 2010 by Joe Kwon, Inc. All rights reserved. Published and distributed worldwide from the United States of America. No part of this book may be used or reproduced in any manner whatsoever without written permission except in the case of brief quotations embodied in critical articles or reviews. For information, address Joe Kwon, Inc, 3 North Lafayette, Marshall, Missouri 65340.

ISBN-10 0-9828659-2-9

ISBN-13 9780982865927

Compiled by Joe Kwon

Edited by Tom Kong

Special Thanks to

Tom Bolling, Joe Bolling, Inja Kwon

Angie Gable, Nicole Beasley,

Zoe Song, and Greg Ashenfelter

Also, a thanks to all those who've shared their own encounters with us to make this compilation a reality, whereby the rest of us may consider ourselves warned that spirits do exist, and not all of them are friendly

Table of Contents

Boogeyman 1
Old Red 4
The Last Conversation 7
The Field 10
Great Grandmother 11
My Protector 12
It's After Her Son 13
Ghost Of My Dead Cousin 15
Sydney? 17
A Shadow Child 18
Erlkin 19
Ghost Roomies 20
At Grandma's House 21
Ancient Army Men 21
Something In My Room 22
Grandma's in the House 24
Father watching over me 25
Lower Lake Lane 27
Ghost Under the Altar 28
My Dead Grandpa 30
The Farmhouse 30
Mysterious Figure 31
New House, New Ghost? 33

v

Ghost Hound	35
Borderland Street	36
Borderland Street 2	37
Borderland Street 3	38
Borderland Street 4	40
Borderland Street 5	41
Borderland Street 6	43
Borderland Street 7	44
Mystery Pasture	45
The Coins	46
The Cowboy	47
How Did You Die?	49
Did You Touch That?	50
A Grandpa's Love From The Grave	52
A Ticking Clock	53
Dakota, Is That You?	54
Was It A Dream?	55
Black Hands	55
Someone To Watch Over Me	56
The Dark Hallway	57
The Tickles on My Feet	59
The Pipe Chase	60
Woman in Black	61
Marion	62
Running to Nowhere	63

Who Was That?	65
A Little Boy	66
Grandma's watching	68
In The Fog	69
Want to Know Who He Is	71
Guardian Angel?	73
Haunted Dream?	74
Jorgie's Guardian Angel	75
Used Cars	76
Let Me Go	77
My House In Waco	79
Darkness in the Hallway	80
Are You Worthy?	82
Shadow Man	84
Fishers of Men	85
Ghostly Children/Ghostly Prom	87
Harry	88
The Carpet	90
El Paso High Is Haunted	91
He is Watching Over Me	92
Knocking	93
Marbles	95
Showering Alone?	96
Someone In the Corner	97
Man On The Couch	99

Floating Boy 100
Irritated 101
Deadly Fan 102
How Did You Die? 102
The Girl In The Doorway 105
Mike's Back 107
Henderson Street 108
A Visit to the Cemetery 111
Confused and Unexplained 112
Lewisville High School Ghost 114
My New Unwanted Roommate 115
Not my Dad 117
The Bedroom Visitors 118
Forgotten 120
An Evil Presence 121
Ghost Girl, Are You A Friend? 122
The Good and the Bad 124
Normanna's Bridge 126
The Growling Ghost 129
The Growling Ghost Speaks 131
Unknown Bruises 132
Unknown Bruises Update 133
Was That A Ghost? 134
Maybe They Celebrate an Arrival? 134
Touched 137

Don't Fear the Reaper	139
Haunted House	140
Someone Else	142
Ghost at The Foot of My Bed	143
Blink	143
Ghost Handprints?	144
My Sister's Closet	147
Red Eyes	148
My Dark Man	149
My Dark Man Part 2	150
My Dark Man Part 3	151
Axe Me If I Care	153
Children of the Railroad	157
It Wasn't Her	158
Angels Everywhere	159
In The Dark	160
The Non-smoker	161
A Face in the Mirror	163
Ghost in the Oven	164
House of Horrors	166
Mommy	167
Baptize me, PLEASE	168
Little Girl in the Hallway	169
Voice in My Room	169
The Rocking Chair	170

Boy that Died in a Fire	174
Apartment 1204	176
Something in the House: The Little Girl	177
Cemetery Incident	180
Oh, That's Just My Dead Sister	181
Black Magic	182
Child In The Hallway Bathroom	184
2:10 AM	185
Madonna	186
The Haunted Doll	189
Man in the Hall	190
iPod	192
Blood On The Wall	193
Bloody Mary	194
Demon Friend	195
Michelle	197
My Cozy Haunted Home	198
Murdered Souls	210
Die. Just... Die.	212
My Grave	213
The Girl in my Hallway	214
The Bloody Little Boy	216
The Wal-Mart Ghost	218
Demon With My Face	220
Ghost House	221

Back and Forth	223
Thirsty Ghost	225
Three Bridges	228
The Lying Ouija Board	229
Angry Motel Ghost	233
The Church, the Priest, and My Son	237
Shawn	240
To Grandmother's House I Go	241
My Doll Shirley	244
Noises, Voices, Sightings, and Phone Calls	246
Back From Iraq	248
The Girl In Red	249
Death Walk	250
Something in the House	252
Don't Let It Get You	253
My Dead Son	257

XIII

XIV

Boogeyman
Llano, Texas

When I was a kid, I used to jump off my bed, not step off onto the floor, because I didn't want the Boogeyman to grab my leg. I would jump as far as I could and keep running.

I eventually outgrew that. I don't remember when it happened, I just remember the days when I used to jump and run.

Now as a parent, I have a son that is afraid of the Boogeyman under his bed. How is it that millions of kids around the world are afraid of the Boogeyman under their bed? Is it instinct? Do kids know something, see something, and sense something, that we adults cannot?

So last night I was in my son Andy's room, comforting him, telling him there is no monster under his bed. He didn't believe me. I could tell by the scared look in his eyes it wasn't doing any good just to tell him nothing was there. I laid down on the bed with him to help him go to sleep.

I felt a bump from under the bed. It was light and faint, but I felt it. I ignored it. It was a spring popping or something. He wailed and said, "There it is, Daddy!"

I shushed him, told him it was nothing. But then we felt it again. And again, harder.

I'm an adult. I'm logical. So I got us both up, and pulled the mattress off the bed. If there was a cat or squirrel or rat or whatever, I was going to put an end to this.

I tipped the box spring up on its side. There was nothing under the bed except Andy's car collection. I looked all over the box spring, looking for a hole an animal could get into. Nothing. I kicked it a few times, to get the springs back into shape. Then put the bed back together.

And ten minutes later it started again.

Andy just clung to me as hard as he could. I didn't understand what could be making the bumping under the bed. I still don't understand. But it was weird, and haunting, and I got scared myself.

I don't remember the bed making any bumping when I was a kid. But I do remember various times through my life, even as an adult, when the bed was vibrating. I could even tell what corner of the bed the vibrating was coming from. I never felt like it was an angel or something good. I always felt like it was something bad.

So I laid a blanket out on the floor where the mattress would have been, inside the bed frame. The mattress I threw over against the wall. I was going to show Andy there was no such thing as a Boogeyman. Despite his crying, I made him lie down with me on the blanket.

How can there be bumping under the bed when I'm under the bed myself? There can't, obviously. But apparently, all that does is force the Boogeyman out. And makes him mad.

First the door slammed shut, so loud I sat straight up, almost knocking Andy aside. Then the door locked. And then I saw him.

The Boogeyman, at least this Boogeyman, is a big guy. I had the impression he was dressed in old clothes, but it was too dark to tell for sure. The horror of being there on the floor with my young son screaming and hanging on for dear life while this thing walked over and stared down at me!

There was no thought of my putting up a fight or protest. It wasn't possible and didn't enter my mind. All I could think of was I was going to die and could I save my son from the same fate.

But the Boogeyman didn't attack. He didn't do anything, except stand there above me and look down at the two of us cowering on the blanket. He stood there so long without moving that I had time to come to my senses a bit. I saw that there was no sign of movement: no breathing, no wavering of arms. His eyes, though it was dark, came across as being paler than his face was.

So I sat, and so he stood, until I got the impression he was waiting for me. I was afraid to move, but Andy was starting to calm down a bit. Not that he wasn't afraid... this was a horrifying experience! But he stopped screaming at least. I started to think. What was the Boogeyman waiting for?

Then I had an idea. Slowly, so slowly, I crept away from the Boogeyman, holding Andy in my arms. We got away from the bed, and I stood up. I went to the mattress and box spring, and setting Andy down briefly, threw them both back onto the bed.

Then I grabbed up Andy and ran from the room. It seems to be the Boogeyman only wanted his spot back, that I had taken away from him. He wanted underneath the bed. I haven't been back in the room again. We're moving.

Whatever you do, don't take away the Boogeyman's spot.

Old Red
Pecos, Texas

I'm the proud owner of a scrubby piece of land down in Pecos, Texas. For those that don't know, Pecos is a little desert town full of tumbleweeds and rattlesnakes. At least, that's the entirety of the impression you'd have by simply visiting my property.

If not for sentimental value, I'd have gotten rid of the property years ago. Having inherited it from my grandfather, though, it simply doesn't feel right to sell it. So I keep it and, other than the annual tax bill I receive, pay little attention to its existence.

On that property, though, rested a little old, faded-out red pickup truck that my grandfather affectionately called "Old Red". This truck was already quite old even back when my grandfather was driving it. He and that truck had a long history. I recall a time when he drove it all the way to California to visit us, and he was pulled over by the police for driving too slow. The officer apparently took one look at the truck and immediately asked, "Sir, you don't even have a working speedometer in that thing, do you?" Grandpa replied, "No." and that was it. The officer warned him to "speed it up," and let him go. For as far back as I can remember, that truck never even had a gas cap. Grandpa simply stuffed a rag into the gas tank to keep the fumes in.

Anyway, there sat this truck. And about five or six years ago (not long after Grandpa passed away) I thought about having it hauled away. To me it wasn't much more than a haven for rattlesnakes and the like. A liability, in property-owner terms. Apparently Grandpa had other ideas, though, rest his soul.

I spent about thirty or forty minutes with a shovel trying to loosen the clay-mixed sand from around the wheels, and got a chain wrapped around the rear axle so I could tow it out. Just then a car pulled onto the property. A young Hispanic man got out and approached me with a disappointed look on his face. He wanted to know how I got the "old man" to sell the truck to me so fast.

Before I could explain that the "old man" was my grandfather, and that I'd actually inherited the truck with the property, the man said something that I had to ask him to repeat.

He asked again, "Are you stealing this vehicle?" But, that wasn't the part I wanted to hear again. So I asked him to repeat it all from the beginning.

He went over it again, "I was here yesterday and the old man showed up and asked me to leave. I was just looking at the truck. It's just rusting away out here. I offered to buy it. He told me no. So, I want to know... are you stealing this vehicle, or did he sell it?"

I started to laugh, but I could tell the young man took it

personal that the "old man" wouldn't sell it to him. And then I asked him what the old man looked like. He gave a very detailed description -- of my grandfather!

I calmly explained that I was the old man's grandson and that I was just looking after the vehicle, and I left it at that. The young man smiled and apologized. With obvious admiration for the truck, and a quick reiteration that he was interested in case the truck was ever for sale, he got back in his car and drove away.

I pondered it for a while, and though I knew Grandpa loved that truck, the young man was right -- it was just rotting away. Perhaps Grandpa's spirit did manage to somehow cling to it, but it was long past time for him to let go. The next day I drove the area and spotted the young man's car parked in a driveway and gave him the truck.

I don't get down there often. I don't know if he ever got the thing fixed up, or if he even still has it. I don't even know for sure if it was the right thing to do, because I don't really know what the young man encountered that day when he apparently spoke to my dead grandfather. I just put it all out of my mind and trusted that I did the right thing. I hope that's the case. For all I know, Grandpa haunted him for it. I say that jokingly. Sort of. ■

The Last Conversation
Garland, Texas

My mother died when I was eight years old. I wasn't prepared for it, even though I should have realized what was coming. I was about as clueless as a kid can possibly be in most aspects of life, and this was no exception.

She had been sick for a long time. So sick, that for the last few years of her life she was completely bed-ridden. The family used a pair of walkie talkies so she could call for help from one room to the next if she needed anything. If she was left at home alone, we'd give one of the walkie talkies to the next-door neighbor. It was just something we came up with as sort of a wireless intercom system.

I remember the day I got called out of class at school to take a phone call. It was a phone call from dad. He said mom was very sick and I should come home. I remember being happy to get out of school early for the day. I remember thinking that mom is always really sick, and then wondering why this day was any different that I should get out of school.

There were a lot of people there when I got home. For some reason I wasn't allowed into mom's room. So, I picked up the walkie talkie off the kitchen table and took it to my room.

I pressed the button. "Mom, what's going on?"

There was no answer.

"Mom?"

Still no answer.

A moment later my oldest brother opened the door to my room and walked over to where I was sitting on my bed with the walkie talkie. He reached down and switched it off and shook his head. Then he turned around and left. That was it. Thinking back, I guess I should have realized at least by then that she was dead. But, I didn't. I didn't even really understand what death was.

A couple of days later we were getting ready for mom's funeral. I remember it being explained to me that mom's body would be there, and there would be music and sort of a church service where we were going.

Back before mom got sick, she'd go to church and she often took her tape recorder and recorded the sermons. I mentioned that I'd like to take mom's tape recorder so I could record this service. The family decided against it, and put the tape recorder away. So, I didn't tell anyone when I took her walkie talkie off her nightstand and slipped it into my pocket to give to her at the funeral.

At the service we each got a moment to go to mom's casket. She looked like she was sleeping very peacefully. I pulled the walkie talkie out of my pocket and tucked it beside her so she could call if she needed anything. No one paid any attention to what I had done. Everyone seemed to just be comforting each other.

When I went to sit down, I pulled my handkerchief from my jacket pocket and handed it to my crying grandmother, just as I had seen adults do in movies I'd watched. I listened to the singing, and to the sermon, and we all went outside for another short service and then we went home.

That night I turned on my walkie talkie and listened for mom in case she needed anything. I fell asleep listening to the intermittent static.

But then her unmistakable voice woke me. I opened my eyes and sat up in my bed. Still gripping the walkie talkie in my hand, I pressed the button. "Mom? You need something?"

Beneath the static, like a distant call, I heard her voice again. As if she were barely within range. "I just need to talk to you about something, honey," she said.

She and I talked for what then seemed like only a few minutes, but looking back I know it must have taken much longer. The exact conversation we had is very personal to me, but suffice it to say that from that night on I understood what it meant when someone dies. For the first time, I realized I wouldn't see her again for the rest of my life. For the first time, I cried in realization that she was really gone. But, I also knew she was no longer sick, and no longer suffering.

I began to fall asleep, so she finally she said goodbye. It's my fault for starting to fall asleep. To this day, when I think about it, I am still so disappointed in myself for getting so tired.

For the next couple of nights I tried to talk to her again on the walkie talkie. "I love you and I miss you," I kept telling her.

After getting home from school the next afternoon I noticed that many of mom's things were gone. Even things I'd put in my room that belonged to her. Her old Sunday-school teaching materials, a blanket that she kept on her lap when she used to get around in a wheel chair, and the walkie talkie were all missing from my room. My grandmother on my dad's side of the family had disposed of these things thinking it would be easier for us to "get on with our lives."

Whether or not the walkie talkie would have ever worked to speak to her again, I'll never know. But, I'll always be thankful for that one last conversation.

The Field
San Antonio, Texas

On a family campout one afternoon I told my family that I was going on a walk around the campsite. I walked behind the camper and onto the dirt road, long worn from feet and cars. I was collecting samples of plants for my biology class, and I saw a huge field full of wildflowers. That's when the noise started. It sounded a little like a prairie dog, until I got closer, then I realized it was an echo.

"Virginia," it was saying. "Virginia."

All I can say is that I must have looked like someone named Virginia, because that's when I saw the woman. She was not familiar to me at all; she was obviously human and looked normal save for her clothes, and her hair; they were so old fashioned.

As I looked at her, she grew older until her skin looked like paper and her hair was just a small bun of white spider silk. I said, "I don't know any Virginias."

I turned curtly and walked to the edge of the field. Then I ran.

Great Grandmother
Austin, Texas

My mother told me the story of how she saw my great grandfather's ghost in the house. My great grandfather died in that house in 1980 or 81.

I was born in 1983. I was about 3 months old when my mother went into the kitchen to make me a bottle. She says that she felt as if someone was watching her. She turned around; there was my great grandfather's ghost. She described him as in his younger years, with his full Marine uniform, but she had no trouble recognizing him.

There are other stories. In my great grandmother's room, she had a lot of paintings on the walls. The paintings were haunted. They would move. Like this painting she had of JFK. My family would say that he would move from side to side in the painting. Also his eyes would actually follow you.

There, too, was the painting of a lady. She had a fan in her hand. Sometimes the fan would be behind her back, other times it would be in front, covering her face, and she would even move!

Funny thing was, the paintings would not move outside of the house, only while in the house. The paintings are at my aunt's house now. They haven't moved since they were taken out of the house 5 years ago.

About 2 or 3 years ago, my aunt placed a tape recorder in the house. She placed it on the floor then left for 2 hours. She came back, heard the tape, and found it now contained hundreds of conversations. Spanish and English! Too much to even focus on one. She even heard my great grandfather's voice on there! Also, there was the sound of someone covering up the tape recorder with a hand. There are plenty more stories, not enough time to tell them all.

My Protector
Lake Jackson, Texas

I am a subtle believer in ghosts, but I have had a few experiences that I cannot explain even to this day. This is one of them.

I had just turned fourteen and me and my mother, stepfather, and two year old sister, and I had just moved into a new house. It was a nice house, fairly new, maybe about eight years old with no history of paranormal activity. Not that I knew of, anyway.

After two weeks of being in the house, there were a few troubling things that occurred. Whenever my parents would be out for the night leaving me to watch my sister, I would hear strange things coming from the office, shuffling papers, the computer shutting itself off and then back on. I would just turn up the television and ignore it.

After going to bed, I would always hear my door open, and feel my blankets being slowly pulled off of my bed.

More annoyed than scared, I would just kick my legs and pull my blankets back up, and then I would hear my door quietly close. I would always look at my clock and it would be the same: 2:04 AM.

But that wasn't the main occurrence. It was about a month into being in the house when one morning I was cleaning the upstairs bathroom. The sink is about five feet long with a mirror just as long that ran up to the ceiling. The bathroom light on the ceiling had a large glass dome, maybe weighing about five or six pounds.

I was cleaning the mirror and was directly under the light. I leaned back to look at the mirror and my eyes were drawn to the dome in the mirror. Suddenly, the dome fell. I watched, frozen, as it fell about six inches when it abruptly flew to the left, silently knocking a picture off of the wall. I stood in shock in the same spot for a good minute before I went to look at the picture and the dome. The glass in the fixture was shattered, but the dome didn't have a crack on it.

I immediately went to my mom in the room next to the bathroom and asked if she had heard anything, but she hadn't. The noise was definitely loud enough to be heard throughout the house, especially with the bathroom door being wide open. I tried to rationalize it, but couldn't. There were no wires attached to the dome that could have swung it in another direction, believe me, I checked over and over, all that kept it in place were screws.

After a while, it didn't bother me anymore. I could have been hurt, but wasn't. I like to think that maybe there's someone watching out for me, protecting me.

It's After Her Son
Houston, Texas

About a year ago my aunt had a really horrifying experience that gives me goose bumps. I am going to give you some background information first:

My cousin's son was about four at the time, but ever since he was a baby he has never been easily comforted. He would always cry throughout the night as if something or someone was hurting him. As he got a little bit older he would wake up in the middle of the night screaming in terror. It got worse as time went by. He never wanted to be alone in his room, and would cry uncontrollably if he was.

My cousin and his wife moved into this apartment and that's when it began to reveal itself. They tell us of many different occurrences. For example, the microwave turns on at all hours of the night, when no one is there to turn it on.

On one occasion, my cousin's wife had one of those old baby swings that you have to wind up in order for it to swing. One night she was in the living room with her son and out of nowhere the swing started swinging on it's own, and not just a little movement by the air, but as if someone was pushing it.

As their son got older they tried to ask him what he was afraid of, but he never really gave a straight answer. He was too scared to discuss it.

My cousin's wife was pregnant with her second child and they were on their way to the hospital to deliver the baby. Well, my aunt stayed with their son, her grandson, whom I spoke about earlier. So, it was just the two of them in the living room watching TV when all of a sudden the air went cold. My aunt said that she felt a numbing feeling that overcame her entire body. She could not move or speak. It was as if some supernatural force was binding her entire body. She said she could feel the presence of evil. This went on for a few minutes and finally it released her.

Without saying a word, she looked over to her grandson and he said, "They scare me too!"

This final phrase gave me the scare of my life. I mean this child has had so many problems since he was a baby and now it was very clear. Whatever it is has been following him since he was an infant. My cousin's wife is from a small village in Mexico. Her family is very superstitious, and they practiced witchcraft. She believes that whatever this spirit is, that it followed her and is now targeting her son.

They have had other experiences following this, but none that I know accurately enough to tell.

Ghost Of My Dead Cousin
Dallas, Texas

Before you read my story, I would just like to add that prior to this experience, I did not believe in ghosts or spirits -- or any kind of paranormal activity! I always thought there was a logical explanation for everything!

It was October 26th, and I was off to Dallas with my Mom to spend Halloween with my Nana. I live in Ireland and the plane journey to Texas took ages! When I arrived at my Nana's I immediately asked to be shown to my room so I could get some rest. My room was directly across from the old nursery, and two doors down from my mom's room. It was only 8:00pm, but I was ready to go to sleep.

Sometime in the middle of the night I was woken up by the sound of a child crying. My Nana had no children, and no neighbors. So, I was very puzzled. However, being so tired I thought no more about it and went back to sleep.

The next day when playing upstairs in the hallway. I thought I heard a bang in the nursery. I looked in the door and saw an old china doll in the middle of the floor. I picked up the old thing and decided to show it to my Nana. She said that she had never seen it before, and that I could have it if I wanted. So, that night before I went to bed I propped the doll up beside me on my pillow and drifted off to sleep.

At 2:34 a.m. I was awoken by the sound of more crying. This time I knew I hadn't imagined it the other night and decided to put an end to it. I cautiously crept out the door and into the hall. The crying seemed to be coming from the nursery. I was very scared at this point, but plucked up enough courage to peek around the door.

When I did this a horrible sight met my eyes. There in the middle of the floor sat a little girl with long brown curly hair. She was wearing a White dress. I tried to be as quiet as I could, but unfortunately the little girl turned to face me.

I nearly fainted in fright because of what I saw. The girl had no eyes, and blood was coming out from her eye sockets. When she saw me she gave me a horrible evil smile and to my dismay she had no teeth, either; just bleeding gums. Then the girl started to walk towards me with her hand out screaming, "Where is my doll?!"

I was terrified for my life! I ran into my mom's room, slamming the door behind me. My mom sat up in bed to see what all the commotion was about. When she saw me, she asked what was wrong and I told her the whole story. I wasn't surprised that she didn't believe me, as I found it hard to believe myself -- but I insisted she walk me back to my room!

When we got back, I quickly glanced at my pillow and to my horror the doll was gone! I was so freaked and demanded to sleep with my mom that night.

The next morning I decided to ask my Nan about what I'd seen. To my surprise Nan believed me and told me what I'd seen before I gave her any details. She told me that a cousin of mine named Laura died tragically in this house after the house was invaded by violent criminals. They beat her to death and then took her eyes out. My Nan says that she usually returned the week of Oct. 24th for her birthday.

Well this is my story, make of it what you will. All I know is that this is a completely true story and I hope nothing like this ever happens me again!

Sydney?
Dallas, Texas

My great grandmother had a cat named Sydney for years. I know she had that cat since she lost her husband nearly 20 years ago.

The cat began getting really sick and eventually died. About two weeks after Sydney died, we went to my great grandmother's house to help her clean her garden up a little. As I was going into my grandmother's home office, I heard a cat meowing from my grandmother's room, which was directly to my left. I looked over and said, "Hey Sydney!"

But as I switched on the light to the office in front of me... my grandmother and great grandmother said, "Whom are you talking to? You know that Sydney died two weeks ago..."

A few minutes after I got what I needed out of that room, I was walking in the hallway sort of adjacent from her bedroom... and I looked down and saw and felt the cat weaving in between my feet as I was going to the restroom... she did this when she was alive, so did she not know she was dead? Anyway, I quickly ran outside and just shook it off.

Was this cat really there, or was I just hearing and seeing things? Well, as far as I know, I'm sane...

A Shadow Child
Houston, Texas

I don't know how to explain this event. This happened when I was a child, but I can still see it in my mind's eye as clearly as the night it happened.

My family lived in the stereotypical creepy house when I was a kid... mystery footsteps, unaccountable noises, feelings of general malevolence, etc. Suffice it to say I never got out of bed at night except in the direst of need. One night when I was in fourth grade, I remember because of a distinctive haircut, I desperately had to use the restroom.

After braving the seemingly endless, pitch-black hallway, I came to the entrance of the restroom.

Directly before me, a sort of white shadow formed. It was a perfect, but featureless, image of myself. It was my shape exactly, from my distinctive haircut to the lace trim of my gown that always kinked up on one side. The white shadow had its hand on its hip. I did not. And it slowly wagged the finger of its other hand before me, forbidding my entrance to the room.

As if I wanted in anymore! I bolted back to my bed and never, EVER, got up at night again.

This event has always puzzled me, because I don't understand why a spirit would appear to me in my own form. And I can assure you of two things: First, the shape was not my reflection in the mirror. The mirror was on the left wall of the restroom, not directly across from me. And Second, I was absolutely positively awake.

The only thing I can surmise is that there were multiple entities in that house, and a kindly one appeared to keep me from encountering one far worse. Still scared the crap out of me, though. ■

Erlkin
Moody, Texas

When I was 10 years old, my dad decided it was time to move us (being myself, mom, dad, and my two brothers) away from the dangers of city living, to a quiet rural existence. This is my tale.

Being out in the country in the plains region of Texas, one can see details for quite some distance. A house a mile away, if you happen to be on a hill, and cows and trucks going out to pasture, and such. I remember hating being out there around the sunset time. That would be when I'd see him: a man-like figure glowing in the golden dusk. He would stand and watch, and he sent shivers down my spine.

During the nights I would sleep fitfully, if at all, constantly feeling like I was being watched. One day, a friend came to visit. You see, I was known for being able to see ghosts, and her grandmother had just passed, so we were holding a small séance so she could properly say goodbye. My friend and her grandmother had ended their last visit with each other harshly, and she regretted it.

Anyway, midway through her farewells, I believe the same watchful presence I had mentioned began to interfere. After that, he became stronger. I would feel his breath as I lay trying to sleep, or he would whisper in my ear. Or play soft pranks during the night. He would say he loved me and he wanted me to go with him.

You see, in Germany where I was born, the locals believed the Erlkin, Elf King, lived in the Black Forest. Think Hansel and Gretel. They were known for taking very young girls who strayed too close, but only if they were pure. I guess he couldn't keep me for I never ventured into the trees in the distance where I would see him.

Now, years later, I sometimes see him when I sleep, but he doesn't talk anymore and I don't feel so watched. One of his brides was taken away I guess. ■

Ghost Roomies
Lampasas, Texas

I moved to Lampasas in the summer of 2000. I hadn't been in my new home long before I realized we were not alone. My husband, my 13-year-old son, and myself were the only ones living in our home. At least, that's what we thought!

Our house is an older home that has been well taken care of and we loved it instantly. One day my son was outside and my husband was at work while I was at my computer doing some paperwork. Out of the corner of my eye I glimpsed a shadow passing by but dismissed it, thinking my son must have come inside to get a drink. As I turned back to the task at hand, once again I glimpsed a shadow passing by me in the hall.

I got up to go see what my son was doing and to my surprise he was nowhere in sight. I looked outside and saw him involved in his basketball game. I asked him if he had just came inside and he told me no, which was verified by his friends.

Since that first time, we have all experienced this movement in the house. Since no harm has ever come to any of us we have decided we have ghost roomies! Now I don't think anything about it and have looked up and watched shadows move past us more times than I can count. Now if we could just get them to pay rent! ■

At Grandma's House
San Antonio, Texas

When I was eight, my family and I used to live with my grandma. We had just moved to town and needed some time to get settled.

One night I was asleep and I woke up suddenly. You know the feeling you get when you are being watched? Well that's what I felt. I turned to the doorway and there was a little boy standing there just looking at me. At first I thought it was my brother but then I remembered he was at friend's house.

I got so freaked out that I hid under the covers. Then I felt him, or something, standing right next to my bed. I refused to come up from under the covers and the next thing I knew it was morning. I don't know what it was, but I didn't sleep by myself from then on.

My grandma's has always had unexplained things happening but this was my first personal experience. ■

Ancient Army Men
Corpus Christi, Texas

My little brother is in a Boy Scout troop, and I got to go along on their trip to the Lexington, a very old warship boat that had a sad and gruesome history.

One night I took a stroll on the deck that thousands of people had died on. The gurgle of the water was music to my ears, and the view was even more beautiful. Then, at that very moment, screams of at least 100 dying souls rang through my ears, the noise was so horrid and loud that I fell to my Knesset and screamed. I then had a feeling that some one was choking me! Then, it all stopped, and I just hugged my knees and bawled.

I used to be a non-believer... Now? I believe. ■

Something In My Room
Pearland, Texas

Hello, my name is Stephanie and I am going to share with you the most terrifying week of my life.

When I was about 6 years old, I had this intense fear of my closet. I always felt as if someone, or something, was in it. I never wanted to sleep in my own room because I was so afraid of it.

This all started the day I found out that the previous owner of my house died in my room. At this time, being only 6, I thought nothing of it. But, I would soon become a believer in the paranormal.

That night, my mom had just put me to bed and I was having a really hard time sleeping. The way my room was set up was my bed was on the opposite wall of the closet, so if I turned on my side, I was facing my closet. My fear was super intense that night. I felt like there was someone in my room with me but I didn't know what to do, so I just shut my eyes and tried to get some sleep. Well that didn't happen.

I made the mistake of rolling over, facing my closet and I opened my eyes, just in time so see a shadowy figure dart across the wall and stop where my closet door was. The figure was odd. If I had to describe it, it looked like a troll shape. It was small, but I was terrified.

I just laid there, I didn't want to move at all, I felt my breathing was too much movement. I decided to look over at my closet once more, and the door begins to open. Slowly, it gets to the point where it can't open any more and slams shut. So what do I do? I freak out of course and run to my mom. That night, I slept in my parents bed.

The next night wasn't too bad, but I was still frightened. Because of the previous night, I decided that I would feel safer if my little dog, Princess, slept in bed with me. Princess was a Pomeranian and really sweet. I was in bed, and I already felt tons safer because Princess was there with me.

I was petting her before I was about to pass out but I remember blinking and opening my eyes again and what I saw scared me enough to start screaming. As I opened my eyes to look at Princess, she turned black, (her fur is really light tan) and her eyes were glowing red. Believe me, I know how weird this sounds, I didn't want to believe it either, but I know what I saw. So needless to say, I kicked Princess out of my room and she slept in the living room that night.

The next night is a night I will never forget. I was laying in bed, almost about to fall asleep, when I hear my name coming from the closet. At first I thought it was my mom, so I listened one more time...nothing. So I roll back over and start to fall asleep. Later I woke to something shaking my bed. At that time, I had a water bed, and it would move easily from anything trying to move it. That night it was moving to the point where I felt I was going to fall off. No one was in my room but me, why was my bed moving like that? I was scared, so I hopped out of bed and started running towards my door. I slammed shut it my face. I was frozen with fear. I just stood there, I didn't want to turn around because I didn't know what would happen to me if I did.

I start to hear my name coming from the closet again. Just repeating, until finally it stops, the door opens and I run to my mom. The whole time I was in my room that night, I felt depressed. I felt like something wanted me to feel that way. Like I was alone and helpless.

Years have gone by and nothing happened. My family and I moved to a new house. One day I remember asking my mom about the person who died in our old house. She told me it was an old woman, she had died in my room, right next to my closet. She was trying to get help, but she couldn't get out of the room.... she was helpless..... ■

Grandma's in the House
Spring branch, Texas

It started on a peaceful night at 1:00 a.m., and my mom and I were sitting on the couch watching TV. Suddenly our back door opened.

My mom and I were pretty scared, so I got up and went to see what it was because she wouldn't. When I got to the back door, no one was there. So I just closed it.

After that I was on the computer, and I heard my cabinet doors open, but I ignored it. Then I heard the dishes being put away. I went to the kitchen to see who it was and all of the dishes were in the same place.

I thought that was pretty freaky, so I told my mom about it, and she said that it was probably my imagination.

After that I went to bed, and woke up at around 3 A.M.

and heard someone talking to me. The voice said, "It's your grandma." I looked around and there was no one there. So now I knew that it's my grandma, and I shouldn't be scared.

From that day on I have seen and heard someone walking around in my house, and I'm pretty sure it's my grandma watching over me making sure everything is all right. ■

Father watching over me
Royse City, Texas

My father and I have had a rocky relationship throughout my childhood, up to adulthood. But, when I turned 25 he came back into my life.

To make a long story short, he came home to Texas to live with my grandma in a hospice to pretty much die at home. They had tried everything, but told us he just needed to be in a comatose state.

The first ghost sighting I had with him was when I left him on the day he passed away. I was at home and was all alone in my room watching TV. I was under the covers and I could feel someone sitting on my blanket. I looked up to see a white mist. I wasn't sure who it was at first. I sat up and put my glasses on and it was my father.

At first I was like, you can't be here. You are supposed to be at grandmas in bed! He just looked at me and leaned down, and it was like he was hugging me. It got cold for like three second and then he disappeared!

Then around midnight my grandma called me to tell me that he had passed away. I said, "I know grams -- I saw him!" She was blown away because she had told me the same story of what happened to her and our stories matched!

Now other things have happened since then, because it's

25

only been a year and I'm still grieving. But, things happen that I can't explain.

I had a friend named Tim who died in combat over in Iraq and I was tore up about that. So, between him and my father, I think they are both watching Over me.

There will be nights when I'll have the remote on my bed far away from me and my TV will turn off and then on again. And I'll have fun -- Ill say, "dad or Tim, if that is you, can you turn on the TV again?" -- and the TV will turn on!

One night I was taking a bath and the lights flickered. There was no bad weather, but the lights flickered and then went off. Now, that freaked me out because I'm afraid of the dark!

Another incident was when I was driving in my car to go shopping and the song I played at my father's funeral was on the radio. On certain occasions it would come on, but only when by myself.

Also, it would be late at night and I would get up to get something to drink and I would see a bright ball of light just zoom past me. One night after the bright ball zoomed past I saw a black figure standing by my pantry door and just casually walk around the corner down the hall and disappear. Now we have a new home only 5 years old, but I heard spirits can follow you and find you wherever u go. But, I don't know.

I have other stories but that is usually what happens on a normal basis. Oh, and one last thing... I'll be laying in bed -- and this is every night -- I will get the feeling that I'm being watched over! But, I don't get scared because I think and hope it's my dad. I saved his ashes in a little sealed wooden box on my nightstand with the angel that points straight to me and watches over me! That angel has moved from on top of his ashes box to the night stand besides my bed and it would face toward me!

Lower Lake Lane
Magnolia, Texas

This all occurs in a house in Magnolia, Texas. I believe the house had two ghosts; there was a child ghost, and an older male ghost.

My younger sister and I shared a room that had a vanity and mirrored backsplash with which you could see down the hallway into another bedroom. (This used to be the master bedroom before my parents built onto the house.) We both had seen at separate times the light being turned off and on in the bedroom at the end of the hall. We also would play with our toys and be looking for a particular part of a set and could not find it. Moments later the item we were looking for would simply be sitting in the middle of our toys with all other toys moved in a circle around it.

Both things my sister and I did not discuss until we were older. When we were younger, we tried to dismiss them as imagination.

These occurrences seem trivial, until one day when I was talking to my mom about it (I was older then of course), she explained to me that she experienced something bizarre in the same room. Before they built onto the house, when it was my parents room, she was in bed and heard the door open then close and the pressure of someone getting into bed. When she reached over to touch my step-dad there was no one in bed with her. I would say it was her imagination, but my step-dad on a separate occasion felt someone sitting at the foot of the bed. Thinking it was my mom, he asked a questions only to discover that he was alone. This all came to light at different times and we had never shared with one another what happened until many years later.

These are just a few experiences with separate people in my family regarding one room in the house. I was young experiencing these things, and talking with my mom and now late grandmother these things run in my family. Apparently, the people in my family are attune to the paranormal. ■

Ghost Under the Altar
Dallas, Texas

Priests and preachers don't believe in ghosts. Ashes to ashes, and dust to dust, and all that. Asleep until the end times and the resurrection. I have never had to really think of ghosts. There is some thought that they are evil spirits and demons, and not the dead. But it didn't matter to me. I am among the living, saving their souls for when they die. Who cares about ghosts and what they are?

Every evening at 9:30 it is my habit to go to the church and pray at the altar. I have done this for the two years I have been in charge of this congregation. It is my duty.

But for almost a week now I have not gone. Because there is a ghost under the altar.

The ghost mimics me. Has anyone ever heard of such a thing? I usually pray out loud. But, kneeling there at the altar a week ago, I said, "Our Father, who art in heaven..." and a voice from under the altar repeated the words after me. Like an echo. A man's voice, an old man, with a quavering voice.

I jumped up from my knees and looked around me in surprise. I thought one of my parishioners had come in to pray too. But no one was there. I settled down after a bit and resumed praying. But the voice started right back in again, copying me.

I shouted at him to leave. I commanded him to leave. And, as best an old man's quivering voice could do so, he copied everything I said, even trying to shout with my same tone of voice.

I left in desperation. I returned the following night, hoping it was gone. But no such luck. I was afraid last Sunday that the service would be ruined, and when I stood to speak I hesitated for an echo. But fortunately, he was totally silent.

I do not know yet if I have to be alone for him to copy me, or if it is the evening time that brings him out. But Monday evening I was back to say my prayers and he was back too, copying me, mimicking me.

My plan is to continue my evening prayers, but to pray silently. I do not know what the reaction will be, if any. But this is odd, and strange, and very scary.

I hesitate to tell any of my congregation, or my superiors in the church...

My Dead Grandpa
Saginaw, Texas

A week after my grandpa had passed away, my grandmother gave my mother my grandfather's watch.

Mom let me see it and made the comment that it didn't work, but when I looked at it, it began working just fine. At that moment for some reason I looked behind me, and there he was... right there smiling at me for just a moment. I was so happy to see him.

About two months later the watch stopped working. I took it as a sign that he was sorry that he had to go. ■

The Farmhouse
Lubbock, Texas

In 2000, my mom told me a story that literally made the hairs on my neck and head stand up on end, and totally freaked me out. It's a little long, but here goes...

My mom was talking to a friend one night, and the conversation turned to the friend sharing how she experienced some paranormal activity in the house she lived in as a young girl. The house was an old farmhouse. When her parents bought it, it needed a lot of work done to it. The linoleum in the kitchen was coming up in certain parts of the floor (kind of like a bubbles) so if you stepped on it, it would make a sticking sound. You always knew when someone was walking in the kitchen. Besides that, the house had an old wood floor. Anyway, whenever she would hear walking or the linoleum "stick", she'd get up reluctantly to investigate but no one was there. Her parents would be sound asleep and she had no siblings.

She would also hear the toilet flush by itself numerous

times at night and sometimes even during the day. No one was in there. The house only had one bathroom and it was right by her bedroom. She could literally see if someone went in or came out.

One day, her dad was tearing up the wood floor in the bathroom because it was rotting out. When they pulled it up, they saw the dirt floor that was under the house.

That's not all they saw either. In the dirt floor, they could see the burnt outline of a human body.

This is not the part that freaked me out... this is:

Once the friend said this, my mom immediately asked where this house was located. When she told her, my mom nearly passed out.

You see, we lived in that house. My grandfather owned it and had sold it to the friend's parents in 1986. In 1984, my step dad was killed by accidental electrocution while replacing water pipes under the house... directly underneath the bathroom.

Mysterious Figure
San Angelo, Texas

These events occurred after my grandfather died, about ten years ago. My grandfather died in our house, just to add a little more back story.

I was asleep in the bed with my grandma and I woke up because I heard this loud talking and very clear words, not muffled. I didn't think anything of it and I went back to sleep.

I was awoken again by the same talking. The voice sounded like a woman talking on the phone. I kept hearing the voice, so I reached my arm over to feel if my grandma was there. I didn't feel her, so I reached all the way until my hand fell off the bed. She wasn't there. So I thought it was her on the phone, and I looked out my bedroom door and I saw this abnormally tall figure, about 7 or 8 feet tall.

I thought it was my eyes playing tricks on me but it wasn't, so I got out of bed and started walking into the living room, still hearing the voice. I got to the living room and there was nothing there: no voice, no figure, nothing. So I called out for my grandma. She didn't answer, so I called her name again. She answered... from the bedroom. I walked in there and she was sleeping in the bed.

I asked her where she was a minute ago. She said she was sleeping. Then I told her I felt for her, and she said that I didn't because she would have felt it. Now people, my grandma was NOT in the bed. I would have felt her. She wasn't there.

I still to this day don't know what it was. My grandma said I was dreaming or sleepwalking, but I know I wasn't. There was something there, I know it in my gut.

To add, we had used a Ouija board in the house after my grandfather died. I don't know what the figure was, but I have my ideas. What Do You Think? ■

New House, New Ghost?
Arlington, Texas

My husband and I purchased our first home in June 2009. The owners of the house had to sell due to her husband passing away and she could not afford the mortgage payment by herself with 2 kids. I am not sure how or where the husband passed away. All I know is he passed away due to an illness.

This story is not a past story, but is a story in the making.

We moved out of an apartment for which we lived in for 5 years. We got settled in our new home the end of June 2009. Everything was great, we were enjoying our new home and were proud to be home owners.

About a month after we moved in, weird things started happening. One night I was lying in bed reading a book waiting for my husband to get home from a friends house. As I was in my own little world of my book, I hear a loud bang on the ceiling that really startled me! After living in an apartment for 5 years I didn't really think much more of it as I was used to the noise of neighbors above us. Then a few minutes went by and I got to thinking of the noise I heard. I reminded myself, "Wait a minute! We aren't in an apartment anymore! The noise came from my attic!"

I was so freaked out I did not want to get out of my bed! I called my husband to find out when he was going to be home and told him what had happened. He came home just shortly after the call and went into the attic to see what it could have been. He did not find anyone or anything. He does not believe in ghosts, so he didn't think much more of it.

A few months go by and we are sitting in the living watching TV and just talking about our day. I was sitting closer to the TV in the recliner and my husband was sitting on the couch. All of a sudden the TV turns off. I jump up and run over to sit by him. There was no power trip, all lights were on. He turned the TV right back on and everything was fine.

A few months later we are sitting at the dining room table eating dinner. All of a sudden the trash can turns completely sideways. My husband, not being a believer, thinks of several different odd reasons why the trash can would just turn sideways. He thinks it could have been a mouse. We do not have mice in our house. Even if it were a mouse, it would have bumped it, not turned it completely sideways!

We have lived in this house for a year and 4 months. Since then we have had several things happen such as me being in the bathroom in the morning getting ready for work and hear my husbands Harley fire up in the garage and shut off. Me being the only one home, I am thinking maybe my husband came back home to get his bike to ride to work since it was a nice morning. I go to the garage and nobody is there and the garage door is still shut! Or at night we would be sleeping at and hear such a loud bang for what we think was at the front door that it awakes us from our our sleep and my husband goes to check and nobody is there.

I believe that it could be the owner that passed away. Maybe he doesn't like loud noise like the TV or he was used to his house not having a trash can in the spot we had it and had accidentally ran into it. I am not sure, but it still freaks me out every time something happens. I am afraid of the dark and always have been so having things like this happen scares me every time. It of course doesn't bother my husband because he is not a believer. ∎

Ghost Hound
Waco, Texas

This story happened to my mom a few years ago.

I was at a family reunion with my parents. We were all at a camp. It was beautiful there. One night, I was asleep and my mom wanted to take some pictures at a city near the camp.

She drove by herself there and stopped by an abandoned looking street. While she was taking a picture of a building, she felt a prickling feeling. She looked around and saw something white appear around the corner.

She was freaked out because it didn't make any sound when it moved. When it came closer, she realized it was a white dog. She stood up and was as still as a statue. The dog came up to her and they looked at each other. The dog was as still as she was, and had blue human eyes and a blue leather collar.

After looking at her, it lowered its head and walked away still not making any sound.

When my mom got back to the camp, she talked to these three other ladies that camped there. She told them what happened, and they said that the man that owns those buildings had a dog that died years ago. That might have been the same dog.

Every time I look back at this story that my mom shared with me, I wonder if the dog was asking her where his master was or if he was just on a moonlit stroll.

Borderland Street
El Paso, Texas

My mom and I moved into my new grandparent's house after she married my dad when I was six. My mother was the bravest woman you could ever meet, and was convinced that one should only be afraid of the living, not the dead. Boy was she wrong. This is the first of many stories I will post, because we encountered many scary things in that house.

From the very start, my mother was not happy with the whole situation of living with the in-laws. She would stay up late at night thinking it was a big mistake. One summer night, at around two in the morning, my mom woke up very depressed and decided to go outside for some fresh air. She was out there for less than 5 minutes when she heard mumbling coming from the right side of the neighborhood and down the street.

Curious of what she heard, she decided to stay and see what was coming. Walking and humming, passed at least 50 hooded individuals holding candles. Some sounded as if they were weeping, while others sounded as of they were praying. My mom felt the hair on the back of her neck stand up for a second, but then convinced herself that maybe this was just a religious neighborhood. She decided to go back inside before these hooded individuals asked her to join them. Later that morning, my mom commented on how weird this neighborhood was. Why would anyone pray like that in the middle of the night?

My grandma and dad turned to look at her with a freaked-out look on their faces, but then told her she was crazy. She knew they were hiding something. Unfortunately, this was the first of many things we experienced.

Borderland Street 2
El Paso, Texas

This is a continuation of my first story, involving not only my grandparent's house, but also the freaky neighborhood I lived in while growing up.

Things were always unusual at the house. The sound of chains being dragged on the roof, of invisible coins being thrown to the ground in the next room, and of people talking in the house when home alone.

The next big incident happened to my mom after she had given birth to my brother. Our little family lived in a room at the very back of the house. My mom used to wake up in the middle of the night to get my brother a bottle. One night, she did her usual routine: went to the kitchen, grabbed a bottle from the fridge and warmed it.

As she was walking back to our room, she saw the profile of a man standing in the dark in the middle of our living room. She initially thought it was my grandpa, but it was three o'clock in the morning. She felt chills and decided to pretend she didn't see it. She started to walk away when she noticed the thing dematerialized and fall to the ground. She freaked out and decided to again pretend she didn't see it, and continued walking to the room.

Then she heard the thing dragging slowly behind her. She thought it was her imagination, so she stopped, and the thing paused as well. She got extremely frightened and started to run, with that thing dragging at her heels. Thankfully, she left the door open and ran in, closing the door. At the same time the thing crashed against it. She locked the door and a second later the door knob started to wiggle. Needless to say, she had a very hard time going to sleep that night, and every night thereafter.

Again, this is only one of the many events that happened in this house. I will try to write about a different event at least once a week. Till next time! ■

Borderland Street 3
El Paso, Texas

When you are a kid, you depend on your parents to help you feel safe. What if you experience something and no one wants to believe you?

We disregard much of the paranormal things children say by telling ourselves that it's just imaginary, but what if you know that what the child says might be true? How do you give the child that sense of security again? Do you lie or tell the truth?

I had just turned six when we moved into the house. This

happened more than twenty years ago, yet I still remember it like it was yesterday. I went to bed one night with both my parents in the room. It had probably been a month after we moved in. I woke up in the middle of the night to the sound of someone screaming at the other end of the house. I figured it was one of my aunts or even grandma, so I was more concerned than afraid. I tried to wake my mom up, but she just told me to go back to sleep.

A couple of minutes later, that one screaming person seemed to have been joined by five more, then ten, then God knows how many more. The sound was loud enough that it should have woken my parents up, but it didn't. I tried waking my mom up again, but she told me I was just dreaming, and to go back to sleep.

As time passed, the screaming got closer and closer to where it was practically outside our room. I looked over at my parents and they were sound asleep. How could anyone sleep through that? All of a sudden, the screams were all around me, yet there were only three people in the room. I was too afraid to move, let alone jump into my parent's bed. All I was able to do was wrap the covers around my head and try to cover my ears. I must have passed out because I woke up the next morning. The only concrete reminder of what happened the night before were the painful scratches on my ears from when I was trying to mute the sound.

I tried to tell my parents what had happened, but they just told me it was a dream and that I needed to learn to distinguish reality from fantasy. I felt all alone. I knew what I had heard; yet no one believed me. I have spoken to my mom about it, now as a grown up, and she apologized for not paying attention to me. She had kept her experiences a secret from me to try to protect me. I learned I wasn't crazy the longer we lived there.

Borderland Street 4
El Paso, Texas

My grandmother on my mom's side and I had a very strong bond. She took care of me before my mom married my dad and took me to Mexico for a year when my mom couldn't afford any babysitters. After my mom got married, my grandma spent a couple of nights at our new house. She wasn't a very superstitious woman, but even she felt the strong entities that lived there. They actually scared her away.

We were extremely heartbroken when she fell ill with pneumonia that was worsened by her diabetes. My mom knew she was in critical condition, so she spent most of my grandma's last days with her. I, unfortunately didn't get to say my goodbyes, but I accompanied my mom to the hospital in hopes that someone took pity on the eight year old with the dying grandma.

My dad usually stayed home and took care of my new baby brother. One night, my dad was putting my brother in his crib, when he noticed some movement out of the corner of his eye. He says the trash can that stood in one of the corners of our little room started to shake, elevated at least three feet in the air and then fell back down to the floor. He was a little freaked, and he saw it as a bad omen. He decided not to tell my mom because he figured she was dealing with enough already.

Early the next morning, we received one of the worst calls anyone can ever receive. My grandmother passed away. Her health deteriorated through the night and the illness got the best of her. We were completely crushed. My dad let us mourn her death for a couple of days before he mentioned the incident.

My mom took it as my grandma's way of saying goodbye. Unfortunately, my mom felt there was still no closure. She became obsessed with the death until my grandmother found a way to communicate yet again...

Borderland Street 5
El Paso, Texas

My mom had a very hard time while mourning my grandmother's death. She fell into a deep depression for a while and it was easy to comprehend her pain.

It was probably about a month after my grandmother passed away, that she decided to communicate. My mom woke up in the middle of the night to go to the bathroom. She opened the room and found a woman standing right outside our door. My mom was a bit shaken, but even though she realized almost instantly that the woman was floating a foot above the ground and her face was blurred in a strange way, she was still not afraid. The hairs on the back of her neck didn't stand and she felt at ease, very different from how she felt with her other encounters.

The woman's hair was long and brown, and she wore a long white gown. My mom tried to get closer to her, but as she walked, the figure floated away slowly. My mom followed her into the bathroom and then vanished when she reached the shower curtain. My mom was dazed and decided to go to bed. She told my dad about what happened the next morning and she convinced herself it must have been a dream.

The following night, my mom had a dream where she was in a field covered in roses as far as the eye could see. She followed a small path and found my grandmother smiling. She hugged my mom and told her she was ok, that she was happy and that my mom needed to let her go. She couldn't rest when my mom refused to go on with her life.

My mom woke up that morning practically glowing. There was no doubt then that her visitor was real, and that it was her mother saying her last goodbye. I love my grandmother dearly even after all this time. In times of hardship, when it's hard to sleep and I'm stricken with insomnia, I think back of when she used to cradle me in her arms and sing to me. I don't know if it's that I remember her so vividly, but I can hear her voice clearly after a while, right before sleep takes me over.

Borderland Street 6
El Paso, Texas

As time passed, we practically expected the sounds and appearances we encountered almost every night. My parents decided to continue living at my grandparent's house for a couple of more years and another baby brother came along in the process. I was twelve, and my mom and dad trusted and expected a lot out of me. Little by little, I became a latch key kid and with time, they started to leave me home alone to watch my baby brother.

One night my parents went shopping with my grandparents and aunts and uncles went out with their friends, while I laid in bed with my baby brother watching TV. My baby brother started to fall asleep, so I lowered the volume. I started to pass out, when out of nowhere came a loud bang from the window right next to me. My brother and I woke up extremely startled and my brother started to cry. It was then that the television started to change channels by itself and the volume went up full blast.

Frightened, I picked my brother up and ran out of the room. I thought I would be safe out of the room, but then I realized our TV wasn't the only thing that was on. It seemed as every single electrical appliance was on! I didn't know what to do, so I ran to my best friend's house and asked for help. Her mom allowed me to stay at their house until my parents showed up. My parents tried to discredit what had happened by saying I had dreamt the whole thing, but my friend's big brother went to my house after I showed up at their house to make sure no one had broken in. He confirmed that every single electrical thing in the house was indeed turned on when he arrived, and he took the time to turn everything off.

I spent a lot of time at my friend's house after that, even

more than usual.

Unfortunately, it took my baby brother a long time to recover. He would wake up screaming and crying every single night until he was about two years old. ■

Borderland Street 7
El Paso, Texas

This is going to be a different story from my previous ones. I will be posting a couple of sightings that I have encountered in my adult life. I've grown up knowing that there is another world around us. After all I went through as a child, I've learned to be more aware of my surroundings. Many of my friends have commented that I act as a magnet to the paranormal, but I believe that I just tend to be at the right places at the right times.

I grew up, went to college and work the graveyard shift at a hospital in El Paso. I will not say what hospital to protect the privacy of my employers and fellow employees. It's nice and quiet where and when I work, but I can actually say I'm not alone.

There have been many times that I've seen a person out of the corner of my eye as I pass by a hallway. I stop to see if it's someone that needs help, and the person isn't there anymore. There have been times that I've been working in front of a computer monitor and I've seen the reflection of someone walking and standing behind me, and when I turn around, there is no one there.

Chairs have moved by themselves right next to me and it sometimes sounds like someone has walked into the room where I'm at and moving things around. I start to talk to the person, thinking it's one of my coworkers. When I get no answer, I find there is no one there.

Nurses have reported sightings of people that have passed away, and cold breezes coming out of nowhere.

I guess it's not hard to realize that these things happen in a hospital considering people pass away. Sometimes it's scary, especially when you're alone.

Just remember, next time you're at a hospital, and you feel a cold breeze, or you see someone out of the corner of your eye, it may just be someone saying goodbye to this world, or someone with unfinished business. ■

Mystery Pasture
Hallettsville, Texas

Three years ago, my family and I made our yearly trip to my grandpa's farm out in the country. As we turned off onto the dirt road, civilization started to evaporate every mile.

When we got there, my dad and I went squirrel hunting out in the woods. We were walking on the grass next to the tree line and my dad stopped and I followed in stopping. We heard leaves being smashed, as if someone was walking close to us. We looked around, and saw no trace of animals, or anyone else.

The sound got progressively louder, until it was as if it was inches away from us. Then the noise disappeared.

Later that night, I was sleeping in my grandpa's vacant guest house with my brother and my cousin. My brother and I shared a bed, and my cousin had her own twin bed close to us. I could not sleep, so I stared at the ceiling. I heard footsteps outside of the room, and they were stomping very loud, so loud it woke BOTH my brother and cousin. The footsteps stopped at our door, and then walked off. We all looked at each other.

The last day we were there me and my 145 pound dog were walking around the front yard and my dog stopped at a certain spot and proceeded to growl and whimper at the spot. I ran to the main house and told my step-grandmother about all of what happened that week.

She told me, "This was a slave plantation long before we moved here..."

The Coins
La Porte, Texas

My grandma told this story to me and I thought it was pretty freaky...

My grandma loves (and I mean really loves) to play bingo. One day while she was at home she was reading a magazine and it had an ad for some good-luck coins, so she sent off for them.

After she got the coins, she would take them with her whenever she went to go play bingo, and she was starting to win. After a while she finally took the time to really look at the coins and see all the detail they had on them.

She said to her horror she saw that on all the coins they had the numbers 666 on them, but you wouldn't know unless you looked real close. And all the coins had it in different areas, they weren't in all the same places; each coin was different. ∎

My grandma got freaked out and she threw the coins in the trash. The next day she found them in her nightstand next to her bed when she woke up.

So, she put them in a jar and buried it in her back yard, and the next morning she woke up to the sounds of coins in a jar rolling around under her bed. She got the jar and threw it against the wall and she started to cry from panic and frustration.

When my grandma pulled her self together, she got up to clean the glass and to put the coins up somewhere so that no one could get a hold of them, but they were gone. She searched high and low in her room but never found them. She said to this day she never found out what happened to them. ∎

The Cowboy
Andrews, Texas

I was about 13 in my parents' house in Andrews, Texas; it's a little West-Texas town with the population of about 10,500. The town used to have money from oil. The oil left and so did the money. Our house was built during the time when oil was still present. It was a large house, about 3,200 square feet. My room was upstairs in between my parents' and my brother's rooms.

One day I was laying on my bed around 7 AM, just thinking about what I was going to do that day. I looked up. and there was a tall Mexican cowboy standing right in front of my bed. He mumbled something to me in a gruff voice.

I couldn't make out what he had said because I was running out of there as fast as I could. I ran into the living room where my mom was. I was crying and told her what I saw and she said it must have just been a dream. I agreed with her so she didn't think I was crazy, but in my mind I knew what I saw was an actual ghost. I didn't sleep in my room for a while and never slept in it alone again.

After a couple months I was very unhappy in that house, so we ended up moving out. But we were in the middle of repainting and rebuilding the porch. We came back every weekend to work on it. One weekend my mom went to the house alone to clean the carpets. She was working on my bedroom and heard someone downstairs so she went down to see who was in our house. She didn't see anyone, so she went back up. She was working and all of a sudden she felt like something was telling her to look into the doorway. There was a tall man standing there. She ended up forgetting about the carpet and coming straight home.

One day my mom and I went to the house together. We were working in the hall outside my bedroom listening to a pop station. Out of nowhere the station changed to a Spanish station. We decided to stop working and go out to dinner. After dinner we came home and went to sleep at our haunted house. I woke up about 11 a.m. I kept hearing some walking back and forth from my room to my mom's bathroom. I went downstairs to see where my mom was to see if she was making the noise.

It turns out she was at lunch with her friends and I was stuck at the house alone. I ran outside of the house and sat out there until she got home. That was the last time I ever went back to our house.

We did research on the house and found out that the builder of the house just happened to be a Mexican cowboy. He also died in the house.

We have recently moved into a different house in Carlsbad, New Mexico. We believe this house is haunted too. Everyone in our family has encountered the ghost at least once.

How Did You Die?
San Angelo, Texas

This happened to me in my house about the same time after my grandfather died and also the same time we started using the Ouija Board.

So, after my family and I started using the Ouija board weird things would happen. Unexplained noises, and with my grandmother also seeing a black figure run from the hall into her bedroom. (Oh also my family didn't know that after you were done using the Ouija board you HAVE to say goodbye or the ghost won't know to leave. I wish we knew that then maybe none of this would of happened.)

When we were using the Ouija board we asked it if there was a spirit in our house. It said YES, and also spelled out a name. Since it was so long ago I don't remember the name but I do know it was a guy's name. Anyway with me being very little (6-7) this was all very interesting to me. So I decided to play a little ghost hunter myself.

I invited my friend who lived next door to me to come over when she did I told her what was going on in my house and she decided she wanted to play ghost hunter too. We decided to write a note to this "supposed" spirit asking it questions like, "How old were you when you died", and

"How did you die". Once we were done we made sure my mom and grandma weren't there. They weren't, as both of their cars were gone. We wanted to make sure nobody that was "LIVING" could write on the letter. So we went into the back room and played for a while. About an hour hour and a half later we came back and the letter had been written on in handwriting that did not match any of my family members.

There were answers to all of my questions like "how old were you when you died," etc. Except one question in particular was not answered. The question, "how did you die" was left unanswered. We wrote many more letters after that asking many more questions (oh and I don't remember the answer to the how old were you when you died since it has been a long time). But, we always asked that same question "how did you die" but it was never, ever answered. I don't understand why that spirit wouldn't answer that question.

What do you think? ■

Did You Touch That?
San Angelo, Texas

This is another story about another incident that happened in my house. If you want more back-story, also read "How Did You Die"?

After writing all those letters and still not being 100% believed, I decided to do one more thing. My friend came over a few days later and I told her what I was going to do. I was going to put 3 different cards (I think they were some kind of angel cards) under a towel in the bathroom in a certain order in a certain way. So we did. My mom and grandma were in the living room. They had NO clue what we were doing.

So we tiptoed into the bathroom (my dead grandfather's bathroom to be exact) and put the 3 cards under a towel in the cupboard very gently and quietly. So we went into the back room with the bathroom door open so we could hear if anyone went in there and opened the cupboard... NOBODY. We went into the bathroom 20 minutes later, looked under the towel and to our surprise all the photos had been rearranged very sloppily and turned upside down. Nobody else knew those were there except my friend Casey who was with me the whole time.

Another story. I was lying in my grandfather's room in the middle of the day talking on the phone. All of a sudden a gust of wind from out of nowhere and made the entire curtain flutter. I asked my grandma to turn down the air, and she said it isn't on. So I listened... She was right. So I walked over to the window to shut it. Window was shut tight and locked.

To this day I think that was my grandfather telling me he will always be with me.

But who was the letter stutter and card switcher? To be honest, to this day I still don't know. Maybe we let out a spirit from the Ouija board, because we didn't say goodbye so he didn't know to go back. I'm not sure, but what I do know is that whatever was there when we were there is still there trapped. I know it!

A Grandpa's Love From The Grave
Pearland, Texas

Growing up my Papa (My dad's father) and I were very close and the older we got, the closer we became. But soon, that all came crashing down. Two days after my sweet 16, my papa passed away. It hit me very hard and I cried a lot, knowing I would never see him again.

One night about two months later, I was having one of my usual night terrors. I have them all the time and they get so bad that what ever happened in that dream usually ends up happening in real life (example if I dream I am being scratched on my back I wake up with scratch marks in my back).

Anyway, on that night I had such a bad one that I woke up. As I was lying there in bed after waking up from that dream I noticed the game chair that I sit in when playing video games was sitting up on its own, which was strange because the only way it could sit up is if someone was sitting in it. As I looked closer to it through the dark, I could see what looked to be a figure sitting in it.

Needless to say, I thought it was one of my sisters messing with me, so I threw my pillow at the chair and told whomever it was to get out. As the pillow hit the wall next to the chair, it fell. I instantly felt a burst of cold air go right through me. After that I noticed a very distinct and familiar smell. It was my papa's smell (my papa had a smell to him that was very distinct, only he had that smell). It was so strong it was like he was sitting on the bed right next to me.

It was like has was watching over me, and it stayed that way for year. I would see him and smell him all the time up until the day of my wedding. That was the last time I saw or smelt him. I was standing in my bridal room waiting for my special day and I smelt him as a cold air went through me. I turned around and he was standing behind me and he whispered to me, "I love you."

And I haven't seen or smelled him since. I know he realized I was ok now and he left me. I loved my papa so much and he loved me too, even in death.

A Ticking Clock
Denton, Texas

I was about 12 when I went to spend the night with my grandpa and grandma. I hated staying in that house, because my family would always tell me stories about when they were young and living in the house, involving ghosts and strange things happening.

I really didn't want to stay the night, but there was no other place to stay, so I had to spend just that one night. I figured nothing would happen since it was only one night, and no one had said anything about anything happening recently.

It was about 11 o'clock when everyone went to bed but me. I wasn't really tired, so I stayed up and watched some TV. I was getting kind of tired, so I shut my eyes for a few minutes, when I heard the door down the hall open. I opened up my eyes and looked down the hall, but saw nothing. I turned down the TV a little and that's when I heard feet walking on the tile. I still did not see anyone there.

I rubbed my eyes, thinking I was just imagining things. But, when I looked at the carpet I could see footprint impressions as they walked across the carpet.

They walked all the way over to the clock above the fireplace, opened up the door to the clock, and stopped it. Then the footprints walked back across he floor, back onto the tile and shut the door again. As soon as the door shut, the clock starting ticking again and had the right time, as if it had never been stopped.

I was so scared that I didn't even sleep at all that night. Instead I sat in that chair with all the lights on (including the light on in the hall) and watched TV the rest of the night. ■

Dakota, Is That You?
Plainview, Texas

My old dog haunts my house. He died when I was 9, so it's been years since he died.

Ever since he died, though, it's been kind of scary. I will sometimes see him a couple times a day.

I'll see a little brown blur in the corner of my eye. When I turn my head to see what's there, the brown blur runs through the wall or just vanishes.

One time I heard him bark in the basement. It scared me badly and instantly gave me the chills. Another encounter I had with Dakota was recently while I was lying on the couch. I turned my head to see if my dog, Baby, was there but she wasn't. I began to watch TV again, and out of nowhere I heard sniffing, like a dog, right in my ear. I thought it was Baby.

I turned around again, but to my surprise all I saw was an imprint in the couch and nothing else. Then I heard the weirdest sound; it's too weird to even try to explain.

I got up and looked at the imprint and said, "Dakota go on and get." Within seconds the imprint was gone as if the invisible beast had risen and hopped down.

Was It A Dream?
Fort Worth, Texas

I have always believed in ghosts and things like that, but what happened to me, I will never understand!

It happened about 2 years ago when I was living with my boyfriend in an apartment. We were asleep when I woke up to something grabbing my legs. I was lying on my back and my eyes shot wide open. Whatever it was had a tight grip on both legs. I couldn't move my arms either. I tried calling out my boyfriend's name but nothing came out. My mouth was moving but everything was silent. All I could really do was thrash my body.

Finally, my boyfriend looked over at me a bit confused. It took him a second to realize what was happening! He started to shake me awake from what he thought was a bad dream. After what seemed like forever, everything stopped and I was almost gasping for air.

My boyfriend told me that it was probably just a bad dream, but I could feel the cold imprint of a hand on both my legs! To this day I don't know what it was. I just hope it never happens again.

Black Hands
Conroe, Texas

First of all let me say that the house we live in is only 20 years old, so nothing real historical could have possibly happened. However, when we were cleaning the land that we live on (an acre) we found parts of an old car underground along with screwdrivers and knives. Who knows what that was all about.

Ok, back to my story, September 30, 2008 at 12:49 a.m. (I will never forget the time), I was in a real hard sleep, when my phone started ringing. If I don't answer by the third ring the fax machine will pick up. Well I woke up on the second ring, and before I could answer it, something made me stop. It felt like my blanket was coming off of me, being pulled toward my feet. I forgot the phone, and pulled the blankets back up to my chin, wondering what was going on.

That's when I saw two floating hands on the side of my bed, up in the air as if they were attached to a person. But of course there was no person. They didn't move, and they were positioned as if they were down at someone's side.

I was so scared I haven't had a good night's sleep in my bedroom since.

This isn't the only thing that has happened here. We have security cameras around our house that are motion-activated. They come on when something passes by. Periodically they will come on and we don't see anything.

We also had a dog that barked constantly. He barked so much we ended up giving him away, and he always barked around the area of the car. ■

Someone To Watch Over Me
Garland, Texas

I come from a large family of eight kids, although my oldest sister and a brother both died before I was born. My parents never talked much about my oldest sister Pat. I just always thought that since she was their first born, it was just too painful for them to talk about.

After I graduated from college, I decided to go to graduate school and I ended up moving to a town close to where I grew up. In addition to going to school and teaching some undergrad courses as a Grad Assistant, I also took another job at a local mall to help make ends meet.

Well, school wasn't what I expected, the people there were snobby, I missed my friends from school, and I missed my family. I felt very overwhelmed with teaching, school and work.

One night, I laid in bed feeling very sorry for myself. I wondered if I should just quit and go back to my parent's... as I cried myself to sleep, I suddenly felt a presence in my room. But I wasn't scared. When I turned over in my bed, I saw the most beautiful woman I have ever seen standing by my bed. She was dressed in white and had a beautiful glow around her! She seemed to be floating and although she didn't speak out loud, I could hear her speak to me with her thoughts.

She told me that she was my sister Pat and that she was always watching over me! She told me that things would get better and to hang in there. She had the most beautiful smile! Then she was gone.

Soon after that, things DID get better and it always gave me comfort to know that she was watching over me. I named my firstborn after her - a son I named Patrick. Of course, he goes by "Pat" after my beautiful sister and guardian angel! ■

The Dark Hallway
El Paso, Texas

This encounter took place when I was 15. It was a nice house, one story with six bedrooms, a dining room, a sitting room, a living room and a kitchen. Since there were many rooms and it was only one story, the house was very long.

There was an extra room that we never used at the other end of the house by itself.

At that time my uncle and aunt moved in for a while. That room was never used until they moved in, and the rest of the rooms were down a long hallway. I have had previous experiences in that house, but this is the one I'm going to tell you about.

One night I was watching The Exorcist with my aunt and uncle, and I was already creeped out because that movie was evil enough. It was about 2 or 3 in the morning as I remember, and I already had an odd feeling about walking to the other side of the house at night back to my room. My mom, step dad and brothers were on the other side of the house as well, so when I got up to leave I said good night and I made my way down to my bedroom.

As I went down the hall and passed the dining room and entered the living room, I started to feel scared about going down this long hallway, because it is the darkest part of the house and you can just barely see anything. But I went ahead anyway, walking slowly, cautious not to bump into anything. In that hallway there is an entrance to the kitchen and once you get to that point there is a little bit of light showing from the outside.

Once I was able to see more clearly, I saw a tall, black shadow walking toward me.

At first, I figured it was my step dad because he was very tall. Because I wasn't able to see, and we didn't get along very well, I was agitated that he was continuing to walk toward me as fast as he was. The last thing I wanted to do was bump into each other because it was so dark. So, thinking it was him, I said, "Hello, I'm in the hallway too!"

He continued to walk, ignoring me, so I said Hello again, and right as I said that I could feel it walk right through me, and it paralyzed me for a couple seconds, like I was in shock. Instead of yelling for help or trying to call my mom, I ran into my room and shut the door, too scared to even talk or move.

Like I said that is just one of the many encounters in my life that I have experienced. ■

The Tickles on My Feet
San Antonio, Texas

My parents and I spent the night at my aunt's. We lived in Austin and this happened in San Antonio, so I guess my parents wanted to wait until the next day before going home.

I had no idea the house was haunted, and I guess that is why my aunt called my parents over to pray for the house. (I was 10 years old and they probably didn't want to scare me.)

I was asleep on the floor near the hallway, my mom was on my right, and my dad was on hers. My aunt and uncle were asleep on their bed (we were right in front of them.) I imagine it was 2 or 3 in the morning. I was cold and I took some of my mom's blanket. Half asleep, I told my mom to stop tickling my feet. I guess she ignored me. I then heard 2 little kids laughing. I was up this time.

I grabbed my mom's arm and as she was waking, we both heard kids running around us. My feet were bare and uncovered, and continued to get tickled. I started crying.

"Stop!", I yelled. She wrapped me in her arms. They kept tickling my feet. The door in the bathroom closed (not hard, very light). Then my mom put me in the middle, her and my dad held me and started to pray for me. Then they waited until I fell asleep.

It was so ugly that night... my mom remembers so much more, and now that I am older I still get freaked out sleeping on the floor barefoot. ∎

The Pipe Chase
Huntsville, Texas

I am a correctional officer for the Texas Department of Criminal Justice.

While on duty one night at the unit, I was doing a security check in the C-5-7 pipe chase. As I reached the end of the long corridor, I turned around to head back to the only door in or out of the pipe chase. When I turned around there was an inmate looking at me. He just smiled at me, and walked through the wall.

I have seen him several times since then, all in the same pipe chase. ∎

Woman in Black
Houston, Texas

My boyfriend and I were at my house, talking in my bedroom. Only my grandfather was home with us at the time, and he was asleep in his room. My boyfriend and I got hungry and decided to go to the kitchen for a snack... this was between 8:00 and 10:00 pm (I don't remember the date) in the autumn.

As we were walking from my room toward the kitchen (you have to pass the living room and have a very clear view of the entry way and front door), I stopped and he ran into me from behind. As he caught my stare toward the front door, he looked up in the same direction. Without a word we looked at each other and went back into my room.

I got two pieces of paper and two pens... the only thing I said was, "draw what you just saw." In about five minutes we handed each other the other's drawing. Both were exactly the same: the figure of a woman in late Victorian dress (about 1900-1910), with her hair up in a bun and a long black dress.

After seeing each other's picture, we agreed that the woman was more like a shadow... she was colorless (the same color as a shadow on the ground), but we both somehow 'knew' the dress was black in color and we could see the dress in great detail.

The 'ghost' woman stood in her place for a moment before proceeding to 'walk' straight through the closed front door. As I said, neither of us said one word about what we saw to the other until the drawings were finished, to be sure one or the other wasn't hallucinating. (I got this tip out of a 'how to catch a ghost' book when I was like 7, and thought this the best time to apply it.)

After we had discussed it (this took only about 10 minutes, for neither of us felt scared), we decided to walk back as if we were going to the kitchen to see if we had been the victims of an optical illusion or a trick of the light. Neither of us saw the figure again.

About an hour later, as we were saying goodnight on the porch, we saw about five medium-sized orbs (way too big to be fireflies and we live way out in the country so city lights are non applicable). The orbs were about 6 inches in diameter, at least, and they hovered all around us, swishing soundlessly before disappearing. ■

Marion
Houston, Texas

When I was about twelve, I was sure my room was haunted. I did a lot of research on this thing and discovered it was a Marion, a ghost that haunts women as they sleep. One thing about a Marion is that if you try to leave it behind it will follow you. I went to my uncle's house and I guess the Marion thought I was leaving it, so it followed me and I know because I was taking a nap on my uncle's couch while they were in the bedroom about twenty feet away from me.

When I woke up, I heard a voice in my head that kept saying, "Don't move. Don't get up."

So I stayed for a while, then I felt a pressure on each of my arms.

I looked down and saw circular impressions in each arm, like something was holding me down by my arms. I kicked, but nothing happened and I couldn't move my arms. So I screamed at the top of my lungs.

I don't remember what happened next, but I either fell or was pushed off the couch, where I could finally move. But there was a red mark on each arm, a cut on my leg, my shirt ripped, and a long purple line that went all the way across my neck until it ended in an x on the side of my neck.

I went to see why my uncle or aunt didn't come help me when I screamed. They told me they never heard a thing. I demanded to be taken home immediately. On the whole ride home that same voice inside my head told me, "Don't look out the window, stay perfectly still, don't move, don't talk."

I never left my house until I was nineteen.

Running to Nowhere
San Antonio, Texas

I was spending several weeks at my Grandparents' new house in the city. I was 14. The house was nice, though I got random chills and feelings of nervousness throughout my stay.

I spent my nights sleeping on the couch in the living room

that was separated from the kitchen by a large see-through fireplace.

One night I got up to get a drink and a snack around 2 AM. I was standing in the kitchen looking at my couch when I heard my grandmother shuffle from her bedroom down the hall.

I put my cup in the sink, and when I turned back, she was already in the living room, grabbing something off the coffee table, with her back to me.

I called to her, but she shuffled quickly back to her room, robe billowing from her speed.

Alarmed, I chased after her, calling to her. I then noticed she seemed shorter than usual and walked with an unfamiliar limp. My stomach knotted.

I slowed for a moment as she rounded to her bedroom doorway out of sight.

When I walked in seconds later, she was lying down, eyes closed. I shook her and asked her what she was doing. She was puzzled and said she never got up. She sleepily told me to go to bed. I did so, and reluctantly fell back asleep.

A while later, I was awakened by someone poking my back. When I turned, no one was there. I did see, however, a finger-sized indention being made into my comforter.

I spent the rest of the night on my Grandma's floor. ■

Who Was That?
Houston, Texas

It was a Friday night, around 12:00 a.m. I was at home alone, in my bedroom watching TV. I wasn't really that sleepy, so I decided to stay up and wait for my older brother to come home from a party. It was raining very hard, floods everywhere, so it was really heavy rain.

I heard my front door open and close, footsteps walk into my bathroom, and stuff fall into the sink. I thought to myself that my brother was finally home after I'd been waiting for him for almost an hour.

I kept hearing things in my kitchen and other rooms of our house. I was watching Jenny Jones now, I was into it, so I decided to stay up and wait till the show was over. When it finished (2:00), my brother went to my room and asked me for the cordless phone. I noticed that his clothes were wet and he made wet footprints on our carpet.

After he went into his room, I sat there and thought to myself, "how was it possible for him to still be wet?"

So, I got up and asked him if he had come home and went out again. He said no. I got very scared and I felt chills all over me. I thought to my self, what where those noises?

Then I started to notice the loud thunder and the bright lightning, which made it even harder for me to sleep.

I laid on my bed and watched my fan go round and round, until a blue light flashed in my room and had me color blind for at least 5 seconds. I looked around, and everything was blue.

When I squinted my eyes real hard and reopened them, I found myself staring at the very first ghost I'd ever seen.

It was a young woman around the age of 26 or 27, wearing a white flowered dress and holding a book in her left hand. In her right hand she held a little girl's hand. The little girl was wearing the exact dress as the lady was.

After that all I remember was that she looked at me and walked out of my window.

A Little Boy
Laredo, Texas

Since I can remember I have always had this ability. I never knew what it was and until now I tended to ignore it. When I was growing up, I would see things and hear things that other people couldn't.

I still see and hear things, but now I'm a mother of a two year old and a one year old, so I try for none of that to affect me in any way... until I noticed my son was talking.

I was on the couch around 1 in the morning and was falling asleep. So I decided to call it a night. I always turn on the lights in my room before I can turn off the lights in he living room, since my room is right next to the living room.

I always put my 1 year old in his playpen, and since my oldest was still up I figured he would follow. I was wrong. Out of nowhere I heard a little boy laugh. I thought it must have been my 2 year old playing with the cat, so I didn't think much of it.

I walked back into the living room and I noticed there was a shadow of a little boy sitting next to my son. I did a double take look and in that split second he was gone. I asked my son who that was and he just looked at me and smiled.

I mentioned this to my sister who happens to live with me, and I asked her if she has ever seen that little boy. She said no, and I was kind of like, ok I guess it was just in my mind.

A week passed by until I noticed my son was playing with that same boy that I saw the first time. I told the little boy that he needs to move on, and that this is not his world and that he needed to cross over. For some odd reason I thought this was going to work.

The little boy vanished and I was kind of in shock that he actually left. Or so I thought.

A couple of days later my brother in law woke up in the wee hours of the night to use the restroom. The next day my sister told me that as her hubby was heading to the restroom, he saw the little boy standing in the middle of the kitchen. Thinking that it was my son, he didn't think much of it until he came out of the restroom expecting to see my son standing there, only he didn't see anybody.

He freaked out and so did my sis. My sister and I talked about this little kid that we both saw and we started to describe him to each other. Turns out that he looks like 5 or 6 years old, with dark hair, and that she has seen that same boy back when I was living at my apartment.

So I'm wondering who is this boy that plays with my son and has been following my family. Scary part is that I feel him when he is close to my kids, but I just can't help but want to find out who this little boy is. And now he appears more often and at all hours of the day.

How freaky it is to have a little boy who doesn't belong in

this world.

Grandma's watching
Lewisville, Texas

My story begins when I was a little boy. My mother and I lived with my grandparents. Well my grandmother became very sick with cancer and had been in and out of the hospital for about a year or so. When it was getting close to the end she wanted to go home. The doctors sent her home and within an hour she had passed away with all her family around her (one thing I need to tell you is that my grandmother was only 36 years old). My mother grabbed me and we ran out of that house as fast as she could run.

Me being so young not really knowing what was happening. We stayed with friends for a couple of nights before returning to my grandparents' house. What happened next would change my life forever!

That night I slept in the room with my mother. We were awakened by a noise in the hall and it was getting close. Then all of a sudden the door opened and there she was standing there in white, floating about two inches above the ground. She was looking right at us. Our eyes fixed on hers and she softly said everything is going to be ok, then faded away.

With my mother in tears, she turned and hugged me as tightly as she could. My mother only had a few years to get to know her mother. She needed closure. This was the first but not the last time my grandmother visited me. I will tell more stories later. And by the way, she died on January 13. It was a Friday.

In The Fog
Dallas, Texas

If you read my first story, then you know I moved into an old house, but it was new to us. Strange things continue to occur, and my sister continues to make up crap that only happens to her.

It was late and my friend's mom was driving me home from cheer practice that ran a little late that night. It was foggy and humid, a horrible, yucky-feel night. My friend, Olivia, was in the backseat next to me when she pointed out a figure in my driveway.

It was slumped over and limping towards the front door. I thought maybe it was my brother. I don't know. I wanted to make sense of this. The only reason you could see it was because of the motion sensor lights outside my house. We pulled into my driveway in time to see this thing dissolve into the door. "What the...?!" is all that ran through my mind.

I invited Olivia and her mom in for a while, but Olivia's mom refused my offer and said it was late and she should start on dinner. By the tone of her voice, I could tell that wasn't the reason she wasn't willing to stay. I talked to Olivia though, outside on the porch for about 2 or 3 minutes. I was begging her to stay the night, that I didn't have a good feeling of staying alone in my room tonight. She shook her head, and said something wasn't right, that she couldn't stay. I begged her again, only to get the same answer. She told me she'd text me later, and practically ran off my porch and into the passenger seat of her car.

I waved goodbye knowing tonight would be a long night. I just remembered, I had forgotten my bag in Olivia's car, which contained my house keys...and my cell phone. I guessed I wouldn't be talking to Olivia tonight, or anybody else for that matter. I knocked on the door quickly, not wanting to stay outside alone another second! My sister, Savannah, opened the door and pointed out that I was late. Just then, a voice I will never forget had said something I would also never forget. "Let me out!" It was a voice that didn't have a gender decided tone. I couldn't tell if it was a boy or a girl, a man or a woman, a child or an adult. I jumped at the sound and blew it off as the wind, since the voice was faint and light and I didn't want to deal with anything paranormal that night.

I hurried to finish my shower because I did not feel safe alone that night. Before I could even get shampoo into my hair, Savannah screamed.

"Oh no, not again," I thought. She did this often, but I turned off the water, threw on my towel, and ran to where I heard the scream. No one was there. Savannah wasn't even in the house.

I saw a note on the table that had stated how she was out with her boyfriend Colt.

What?! She left me here in this death trap we call home, alone? My mom and dad were working overtime so we could move.

I re-read the last line over again, "Call in emergency. Any emergency." That meant she was expecting a paranormal experience tonight, and she left me! So, naturally I called her, begging her to come home as quickly as possible!

I changed into my pajamas and curled up in a ball under my covers waiting for Savannah to return home.

Where's my brother? You may wonder. His was at his buddy's house.

"Jenna," the voice spoke my name.

My head popped up and I began to shiver. A gust of cold air had blown through my room.

"Leave me alone, please!" I begged of the spirit. "Please, just go away! Please!" I was crying now.

"Jenna," it said again.

The next thing I remember, Jeremy, my brother woke me. I was lying on the floor in the basement outside his bedroom door. How did I get there? I have no idea. But I believe that thing we saw in the fog had something to do with it.

Want to Know Who He Is
Klein, Texas

I first started seeing just glimpses of something. Then one night while I was in my room getting ready for bed, he walked by my door and looked at me. Of course I freaked out, thinking that someone had gotten into my home. My husband was at work but on his way home so I called him on his cell phone (frantic). He told me to calm down and get my gun! I checked the house and there was no one here.

My husband arrived home and checked the house himself, being that he is a police officer. I finally calmed down and went to sleep after taking a muscle relaxer (I was that terrified).

I started to see him more often after this incident. He would be standing off beside me, or would pass through the room I was in. I had been told by several people not to communicate with him, because it could be evil. In spite of their advice I felt it appropriate to say something. I sat on my bed with a cover around me shivering with fear as I started my conversation. I asked him he was here, and if there was something I could do to help him. I asked him to never touch my children or me! I waited for a reply terrified of what would happen.

About the time I was ready to think he could not communicate with me, my computer came on with the word "HELLO" bouncing around! My computer was in sleep mode and would never come on unless I restart it or take it out of sleep mode. I was about ten feet away from it at the time.

My husband and I decided we would not tell my children. But to my surprise, one of my children had been experiencing the same thing I was, but was afraid to tell anyone. I think he thought I would think he was crazy, because I thought the same thing.

Since then, it has made it's presence known to everyone except my husband, but then again, my husband is never home.

He works all day and an extra job until midnight every night during the week. My dog even sees him: Patches watches someone walk around our home. I see him raise his head and move it as whatever he is watching moves from one side of the room to the other.

He even picks at the kids - when they are doing their homework he pushes their pencils off the table (they don't roll they get pushed without rolling, almost like sliding).

I've taken my house shoes off when getting in my bed and in the morning they will be turned around so I can just slip my feet right into them. I have a big stand-up mirror in my bathroom where I pluck my eyebrows... one night I was doing this and he tilted the mirror so I couldn't see. The mirror is hard to tilt. I keep it tight so it won't wiggle around. I'm not afraid, and my children say they are not afraid either but we are very curious...

Guardian Angel?
San Antonio, Texas

This happened in the year 1961, my oldest son Daniel was only about 1 year old. My wife and I had only been married a little over a year and I was working the second shift, my wife and my son Daniel were at home by themselves.

The time was about 2:00 a.m. I received a telephone call at work for me to go home as soon as possible, my wife's voice was shaking and she was scared. When I got home I sat down with her and she began to tell me what had happened that night.

The night was hot and humid and I had purchased a small air conditioning floor unit and placed it in the bedroom; my wife told me that she was fast asleep and the baby was lying next to her on the bed.

For some unknown reason, she awoke and saw my son standing next to the a/c unit like trying to hide behind it. My wife told him to please come to bed and lay next to her and as she started to pat his side of the bed, she realized he was there already. She turned and looked at the a/c unit and still saw my son there. The apparition started to disappear from the feet up until he totally vanished.

After my wife got over her shock of seeing two babies is when she called me at work. To this day I think about her experience and wonder if that other baby was his guardian angel or what? ∎

Haunted Dream?
Beaumont, Texas

Okay so for about two weeks now I've been dreaming about this baby. It looks pale and dead and something tells me it's an unborn older sibling.

It scares me to death because its eyes are pure red and it walks around in my dreams.

I always wake up hearing things moving around my room and I'm sweating and crying. Then I hear a baby crying. It's been happening every couple of nights, always at 3 o'clock.

This was freaking me out! I asked my mom if I had an older sibling that died as a baby, but she gave me a weird look and it took her a while to say no and she kind of looked upset. I think she knows something about this dead baby that's haunting me.

If anyone has any similar experiences and knows what's happening please comment. ∎

Jorgie's Guardian Angel
McAllen, Texas

One day I went to my cousin Erica's house and was talking about paranormal shows on TV. Ghost Hunters, Ghost Adventures, etc. And my cousin Erica said, "Jorgie (her 4 year old son) saw a ghost." I said, "Really, no fair. What happened?"

To give you a heads up, I barely see my cousins at all, so she didn't tell me this until like three weeks later.

This is how Erica explained it to me:

Three weeks ago, Jorgie's paternal grandpa died. When Jorgie was at his house with his dad, Jorgie's dad said Grandpa wasn't eating, and was sleeping a lot lately. And on that day, he wasn't moving at all.

It looked like he was sleeping, but he slept all day. They wanted to take him to the doctors to see what was wrong. But, when they moved him he didn't wake up. They called 911, and the ambulance came, took him to the hospital and later on they pronounced him dead. He and Jorgie were so close.

Erica was on the computer, and Jorgie was in the living room getting ready for school. Out of nowhere, he just jumped up and gasped. Erica asked him, "Que paso, Jorgie (what happened?)"

He said, "Yo miro welo (I saw grandpa)!" My cousin said, "Tell him you love him, Jorgie."

"Te quiero welo," he said. Then Erica heard Jorgie making a conversation about school with his grandpa. Afterwards she asked him, "What did he tell you, Jorgie?"

"That he loves me and that I have a good day at school."

And my cousin Erica then told him his grandpa is his

guardian angel. ■

Used Cars
Tyler, Texas

I heard this story from my cousin. It is true and will make you think twice before buying a used car.

Basically, my cousin had a friend who had a boyfriend. They all lived outside of Tyler, Texas, where the landscape is a little hill country, with rolling hills, trees, and winding roads.

The boyfriend of my cousin's friend had an old used truck, and he would take his girlfriend for rides and such. One day, the girl felt something and looked down at her leg where she saw a hand that quickly moved.

Confused, she asked her boyfriend if he had just touched her leg and he said "no". This was creepy enough for her. The boyfriend didn't really understand until one day he was looking in his rear view mirror and saw someone else's eyes looking back at him!

This was bad enough, but as the strange happenings progressed, he would feel something taking control of his steering wheel, like other hands at times. He would lose control of the old truck because something else was trying to steer, perhaps even wreck him on the winding, tree lined country roads.

Needless to say, he got rid of the truck. Now, doesn't this make you want to do a little vehicular history research before buying a car with a past? ■

Let Me Go
Midland, Texas

Since this happened I have asked my friends and coworkers if anything similar has happened to them. Unfortunately, some have an explanation more terrifying then the one prior to it.

When I moved out of my mother's house I lived with my boyfriend. My mom worked really early in the morning and I had a younger sister, about 5, that I would have to awaken and take to day care for the day. Every morning at 4am I would drive to my mom's house while she got ready, and sleep on the couch until it was 7am and got my little sister ready for day care. One morning my mom had left at about 4:30. I had settled in on the couch and drifted off to sleep.

I awoke, startled by something. Something that hadn't made a sound, something that hadn't moved at all, but something was there. It was just a presence that I instinctively knew was there.

It's normally cool in my mom's house. If it wasn't, I had already turned on the air conditioner to make it so. But now, the air was thick and warm... constricting. I tried to ignore it. Yet, every time I closed my eyes again, I felt like whatever it was, it was moving closer to my side.

My mind whirled with what it could be. It was hard to concentrate with the air this way, and now there seemed to be a fog about my head like I couldn't focus.

I summoned up my courage and pulled my arms up to the

sides to lift myself up and look around. Nothing happened. My arms kept to the sides of my body, and my back remained flat on the couch. I couldn't move!

Panic swept through me quickly and my breathing became short and heavy. But, not because I couldn't move... there was a pressure on my chest. It was light at first, but becoming heavier and heavier. I couldn't see anything holding me down, but I could feel it. I felt it was a woman, old and withered. Ancient. Angry. She was hideous. And I couldn't see her. She was just there.

I opened my mouth to scream or call out. Something to break this unearthly silence, while the hag tried to strangle me, or whatever she was trying to accomplish. No sound. My mouth was moving, but no sound. My vision was blurring and fading and darkening and I guess I passed out. I awoke again gasping and sat straight up on the couch. I sat straight up! I could move!

I searched the living room. Nothing. I shivered. I was drenched and the air in the room was cool again. I got up to turn off the air conditioner. My muscles ached and my chest hurt. I held myself, I couldn't help it I was scared. It had to have been just a dream.

But why did I ache? I went to the bathroom to examine myself. Paler than normal, and dark circles worse than ever. I would chalk it up to a dream, if it hadn't been so vivid, if my surroundings weren't so precise, and if not for that long scratch from just beneath my left breast extending down my side. ∎

My House In Waco
Waco, Texas

I moved into this house in August of 2009. This was my sophomore year at Baylor University and I had two other roommates. This house was not the first house to be built on the site it was at, you could tell by the location of the front walkway and the way the driveway went off past the house into the yard.

The first time I went into the back bedroom, I started talking to no one at all. Last I checked I wasn't schizophrenic so I felt it odd that I would be compelled to speak to air. I hurriedly decided to pick another room. My roommate who stayed in that room could find no explanation as to why his posters wouldn't stay on his walls. After a couple of weeks, none of us could figure out why his door would always crack open an inch or two, even when we placed chairs against it.

Our fears were usually forgotten after a beer or six, so when my girlfriend woke me screaming the most horrifying scream I'd ever heard, all past occurrences sprang to mind. She had been sleeping next to me when she woke to feel hands around her throat. She opened her eyes to see "the most hateful and evil eyes she had ever seen".

I cannot describe her fear any other way as to say that I couldn't move or speak when she started screaming. I was literally scared stiff. Gradually she calmed down enough to sleep there again. Two weeks later in the same situation (same girl), I woke to see a hand waving in front of my face, in between her face and mine. I sat up so fast it woke her and she got scared at the rate my heart was beating.

I tried to focus my eyes but there was nothing there when I did. I won't go into detail as to the many times my cat came running out of that back room with her hair all frizzed up. Cats can be said to be insane as it is so that isn't much proof.

But, the time I came home and found my girlfriend huddled in a corner with her head on her knees, crying, I do feel is admissible. She could only say that she was too afraid to do anything else, and she didn't know what was wrong with my house.

My roommates both moved out 3 months before the lease was up. I stayed for lack of the funds to move out. But back to the door that wouldn't stay closed, we literally shoved a chair under the doorknob only to find that as soon as we weren't looking, it had opened again.

This story is true and I hope my experiences help some one realize what is happening in their house too. ■

Darkness in the Hallway
Amarillo, Texas

I was just a kid, maybe seven or eight years old when this experience happened.

I grew up in Amarillo, Texas, loving scary movies and sharing frightening tales with friends and family; and believing that ghosts and goblins existed, but never having experienced anything supernatural, except for this one and only time. I am grateful for that.

On this specific Friday evening, my family and I spent time watching a marathon of scary movies like we usually did every Friday night. Typically, I was allowed to stay awake into the wee hours of the morning during this "family" time, but for some reason, on this particular evening, I fell asleep amid the marathon.

Then, strangely enough, I awoke in the middle of the night on the living room couch with a pillow under my head and a blanket over my body. Apparently, my parents put me there when everyone went off to sleep. The couch was placed against the wall that was aligned straight with the hallway; and the hallway light was always kept on during the night.

As I lifted my head up from the couch, slightly confused as to where I was and still disoriented, I turned to look in the hallway and saw a pitch black figure standing there, as still as a statue. The figure was eerily tall, almost as tall as the 10-foot ceiling, and extremely thin, similar to a silhouette of a shadow.

I instantly freaked out, my heart started to rapidly palpitate a million miles a minute, my body got shivers from the top of my head to the tip of my toes, and I was on the verge of freezing up from the fear.

I rubbed my eyes, hoping that the scary movies I've watched earlier in the night might have been the reason I saw the figure, but when I reopened my eyes, the scary figure was still there, exactly the same as before; it didn't even move an inch. I knew the figure was real!

I instantly pulled the blanket back over my head and cowered in fear as beads of sweat peppered my body. I briefly contemplated yelling for help, but once I did, I thought the demonic figure might disappear and when my family came out to get me, they might have thought I insane; so instead, I tried to save myself the potential embarrassment, and laid on the couch in silence, barely able to move except for the light trembling I was experiencing from the sheer fear of the darkness in the hallway.

For the rest of the night, I kept the blanket over my body and tried to listen to my heartbeat to calm myself. This technique worked because eventually, I drifted off to sleep, only to awaken to the silence of my house and the sunlight streaming in through the living room windows. The black figure was gone.

I spent some time asking each one of my four sisters and my parents if perhaps, they spent some time in the hallway last night, but they all said no, looking at me like I was off, and some even explaining it was probably just my imagination.

The "demonic" black figure never reappeared, and though I was only left with the possibilities of why it was there, I choose not to question it too much, preferring the ending to be like this. ■

Are You Worthy?
Fort Worth, Texas

In 2007, I moved in with my husband to be. The house belonged to his grandparents who bought it brand new in 1961. They passed away in 1993 (grandpa) and 1996 (grandma).

One night, we had just laid down to go to sleep. About 5 minutes after doing so, the bedroom lamp on my side turned on by itself. The lamp has 3 settings: low, medium and high. The lamp had turned on to high. Anyway, we both looked at each other and just shrugged. I leaned over and turned it off. Not even a minute passed by and it turned on again on the highest setting. I looked at my fiancé and he was just as dumbfounded as I was. I turned it off again and guess what? It turned on a 3rd time, on the highest setting.

My fiancé suggested I unscrew the light bulb, so I did. I told him if the lamp turns on again with the bulb unscrewed, I was leaving and not coming back!

It didn't turn on again that night, but it has a few times since then. With the bulb screwed in of course.

About a week later, my fiancé was at work (he worked the night shift). I went to bed and was awakened by someone leaning on the mattress on my side of the bed. It was as if someone was either sitting on the edge or leaning in to look at me while I was asleep. There was no one there and I was the only one home. Anyway, I felt the mattress slowly "go back" as if someone got up from sitting on it.

The next night, the fiancé was at work and I had gone to bed. This time, I fell asleep with the lamp on low because the house was freaking me out! I woke up to something or someone shaking my leg as if they were trying to wake me up. Again, no one there.

Along with those experiences, I've heard footsteps and things come up missing when I know I set it somewhere and it's gone. I come back 5 minutes later and it's there.

This next experience happened to my 8 year old stepson. We got up one morning and he was asleep in the recliner in the living room. We had put him in his own bed the night before. I asked him if he had trouble sleeping and that was why he was in the recliner and his response chilled me. "No", he said, "Someone carried me in here."

Come to find out, my husband's grandmother died in our house in that very same recliner. Why he kept it, I have no idea but it's gone now! I truly believe she was making sure I was worthy of her house and her grandson. I'm guessing I passed the test! Thanks for reading my story. ■

Shadow Man
San Antonio, Texas

A few months ago I moved into a large house down the street from where I lived before. Someone (perhaps a neighbor, but I never saw him again), walked past me in the street and said, "I wouldn't be living there if I were you."

I just looked at him like he was crazy (mainly because I thought he was), and just ignored him. Shortly after getting moved in, though, as I went to bed (after going through the house and turning off all the lights), I heard this weird noise downstairs. I went to check out what it was making the noise. I got to the kitchen and as I turned around something just appeared in the corner of the room. The best way to describe it is it was like this big black shadow, but it was standing. It was at least 7 feet tall, and just staring at me.

I couldn't move, and it was coming closer and closer. I was frozen with fear, but before it touched me, it just disappeared. This has happened several times since.

I haven't lived here long, but I am afraid of what is still coming. ■

Fishers of Men
Rockwall, Texas

I'm not sure what they were. Ghosts? Angels? I don't know. I just know they weren't human.

This happened one summer at an older brother's house in Rockwall, Texas, when I was around 14 years old. My brother had a house on a small lake, and I frequently enjoyed taking his boat out fishing.

It was broad daylight, at around 10am. I had just gotten into the boat, which was just a small aluminum boat large enough for three or four people. The boat was still out of the water. I hadn't put it in the water yet, because I had just discovered a couple of porn magazines under one of the seats. I was sitting there thumbing through the pages looking at the pictures.

I felt pretty safe from being caught because my brother's yard, like all the other yards around the lake, was very long and wide open. There was no way for anyone to get close enough to see what I was reading without me seeing them first. I would have quickly noticed anyone within a hundred yards of me. At least... that's what I thought.

I'd been in the boat for only a moment, and every few seconds I had been nervously looking around to see if anyone was nearby. Suddenly I glanced up and from out of nowhere there were two men standing right next to me at the edge of the boat! They were neatly dressed in very modern, dark suits. The simply appeared out of nowhere.

I sheepishly tucked the magazine down under the seat again, knowing they had already gotten full view of what I had been reading. They were THAT close.

I was simply in awe that these two mysterious men could suddenly just be right there without me seeing them walk up. I mean, they simply weren't there a second ago, and then suddenly there they were!

One of the men spoke to me. He asked me point-blank, "What are you doing?"

What could I say, except the obvious: what they already knew from observation. I tried to make it sound as innocent as possible without lying. I told them I was just thumbing through one of my brother's magazines.

He then said they liked to fish, and asked me if I could tell them where the best locations were. I pointed down to the far end of the lake that was surrounded by a heavily wooded area and told them that's usually where I caught the most fish. I mentioned that it would be a long walk for them, and that it's better if they have a boat. He thanked me, and the two men glanced at each other. The moment they broke eye contact with me, I quickly glanced down to see how visible the magazine was that I had blindly tucked back under the seat. I didn't want to be obvious about it, though, so I didn't even get a full glance at the magazine before I looked right back up at the two men. Only, in that very instant they both simply vanished. Gone. No trace of them whatsoever, they simply vanished as quickly as they had appeared.

This was not a dream, nor was I on any type of drug or medication whatsoever. This really happened and I've never forgotten it and I'm still amazed by it.

Ghostly Children/Ghostly Prom
Sanger, Texas

This happened at my girlfriend's house in Sanger. The first part of the story happened to her and her family, and takes place when we were 13, and the second part involves me, when we were 17.

Part 1: Ghost Children
When Elaina first moved into the historic house of her mother's dreams, she was home alone, sitting in the living room. Her brother walked by and she didn't think anything of it. 15 minutes later, her mom comes home with her little brother, whom she had just picked up from school.

One night, Mrs. Wilson was making dinner and was squatting down to get a pan out of the drawer below the oven and saw a small boy out of her peripheral vision. She did a double take and the boy was gone.

The whole family hears whistling all of the time (even on windless days, so it's not the wind, and they've checked the A.C but it's not that either).

Part 2: Ghost Prom
On the night of the prom (we were then 17) I arrived a little early and Elaina wasn't done getting ready, so I waited at the foot of the stairs, and a girl (who wasn't Elaina) in a dress walked slowly down the stairs, planted a kiss on my cheek, and continued to walk around the corner (no sounds of windows or doors opening were heard). A few seconds later, Elaina walked down and I asked who else she had over. She said no one, so we checked the house, but didn't find a trace of the girl.

Late that night, I was asleep. I awoke to a burning sensation on my cheek where the ghost girl kissed me. I went to the bathroom, but my cheek looked fine. The prom ghost hasn't appeared since.

We did a bit of research on the house, and found out that a young boy died on the property. We checked house, school, county, and death records, but couldn't find anything on the ghostly prom girl. ■

Harry
Quinlan, Texas

A friend and I moved in together to help each other since we were both single parents. She had a son, 12, and I had two sons, 11 and 13, and two daughters, 8 and 7.

The house we rented was a five-bedroom right on a lake. We were shocked at the rent only being $250 a month, but we thought it was because my friend worked with the lady who owned the house.

She told us that she, her two sons, and her now-dead husband had built the house. Shortly after finishing it, Harry died of cancer.

She laughed and said, "I hope you're not afraid of ghosts. Harry is still here."

Both my friend and I had dealt with ghosts before, and I joke about having my mom and dad both with me all the time even though they both are dead. But, that is another story!

While moving in, several strange things happened. The

first weekend we were there, kids being kids, Verne and I had problems getting the kids to settle down for bed. They all five kept running up and down the stairs. After three or four attempts to put them down, I heard a lot of noise coming from the back yard. I started downstairs to check it out.

Just as I stepped on the last step, I realized it was broad daylight at midnight. I looked out the window in front of me and could see the lake in our back yard. A man in a Panama hat, tan pants and a bright blue shirt was standing looking out over the lake, waving to some people in a sailboat.

I shook my head and it was dark again. I returned to bed in shock. Only minutes after getting cozy the kids started down the stairs again. I heard dishes rattle and a dish break, kids scream, then rapid movement back up the stairs.

I jumped up and opened my door. I went into the girls' room to find nobody there. In the next bedroom I found all five kids piled up in one bed. They told me two plates and two forks flew past them at the bottom of the stairs and hit the wall, then two forks stuck in the floor of the last step. Then there was light outside like it was noon and a man was standing in the back yard pointing at the house.

By this time Verne was up and laughing at them. It was only Harry, she told them with a wink at me. We all went downstairs to check it out. Nothing was broken, no forks in the floor, everything was just as we left it. We sent the kids back to bed and Verne and I sat down at the table for a smoke. I told her what I saw and heard. She told me she had seen the same thing the morning before when she was leaving for work at 4 a.m. I did not tell her what this man looked like, she told me!

We lived in that house for three years and do I have lots of tales from it. One couple moved in after we moved out but only lived there three weeks. They said there was something in that house that was not alive. The house stood empty for over a year, then was sold and still nobody has lived in it.

The new owner tore it down. He said after it started falling apart strange things started happening. I will never forget Harry. ■

The Carpet
Robstown, Texas

This is a story that my mom told me that happened to her.

My grandfather came across some carpet that had been thrown out. It was in good condition and so he took it and brought it back home. He told my mother that he was going to install it in her room, and she was so excited.

My grandfather spent most of the night installing the carpet in my mom's room. She ended up falling asleep with her mom.

When morning came my mom rushed upstairs to see how it looked, only to find that there was no carpet. So she ran downstairs to ask my grandpa about the rug, and he said the carpet wasn't as good as he thought, so he had to get rid of it.

Later that day my mom overheard my grandma and grandpa talking. She heard him tell my grandma that last night when he went down stairs to get something to drink he heard crying coming my mom's room. He rushed back up to see if mom was up there and had maybe gotten hurt on some tools or something.

When he open the door he saw, instead, an old man in a wheelchair with his head in his hands, sitting by the window. So my grandpa freaked and tore out the carpet and threw it away. ■

El Paso High Is Haunted
El Paso, Texas

Well I have never seen a ghost before, but this story is worth researching.

I live in El Paso, Texas, and there is this school that's been around well into the early twenties and a lot of people around town say this place is haunted.

Stories range from a cheerleader who committed suicide after her boyfriend died at football practice to when the second World War was happening and our soldiers who died in combat were put in tunnels underneath the school to be put to rest at the Army cemetery. There were even stories of satanic worshipping in the tunnels. And not to mention custodians that also committed suicide.

Everyone has heard of the ghosts and this story deserves attention. This school is on a side of a mountain and it looks like House on Haunted Hill at night. Come and check this out. My friend is a cop and he works for the school district and he claims that the alarms go off at that school at night, and he goes to see what's going on in there with other police officers, and they go track the motion sensors in the school and claim they would hear foot steps of someone running but no one is there and alarms would go off on all four floors.

The whole city is in fear over this place. There are other old schools that are haunted as well but none so haunted as El Paso High. ■

He is Watching Over Me
Ft Worth, Texas

This is not a scary story, but more of a touching story of a grandfather watching over his granddaughter.

My grandpa was one of the most important men in my life. He took care of me when my parents were working or going to school. When I was younger, he gave me a Teddy bear that I cherished forever. He passed away in March of 2003 and I was devastated. His death was sudden and very unexpected.

I have had dreams of him since he passed, of us just sitting and talking. And I have woken up swearing it was real. The dreams temporarily stopped about a year and a half ago. But, everything else started about a year ago when my husband and I got married and moved into our new house.

The first occurrence was at my wedding. I was in the room getting ready to walk down the aisle, and the photographer came in and took a picture. When I viewed the picture, I noticed what looked like an odd shadow standing next to me. It almost looked like someone standing there, just as if they were going to give me away. I looked at the rest of the pictures and I found others that had orbs, and even more with strange shadows just like the first one.

After the wedding we moved into our first house together. I had a box with some of my grandfather's things in it; such as the bear he gave me, some of his old rings, and the keepsakes from his funeral. That box was one of the first things I moved in, and I took it straight to our room and put it in the closet. We left to go get another truckload and when we got back to the house, that bear was in the living room. I thought maybe it had fallen out of the box, but I had to walk back through the living room, so I would have noticed it being there.

I then started having the dreams again, even more vivid and real than before. There hasn't been anything else, but I can't help but think this my grandpa's way of giving his approval of the way my life is, and I think he is watching over my house and protecting us.

Knocking
Austin, Texas

When I was a kid, around 11 or 12, I was in the bathroom by myself and for the fun of it I tried to call Bloody Mary. I turned the lights off and said her name three times. I waited for about five minutes but nothing happened, so I went to bed. Later around 3 a.m., I woke up with a really bad feeling, like something was wrong and I shouldn't be there. So I got up and went to my younger sister's room and got in her bed.

After three minutes I heard a loud knocking in my room; it kept getting louder and louder. Then it stopped. But, being too afraid to get out of bed, I just stayed there until morning.

In the morning I went to my room and every thing was fine until I saw my little mirror on the floor with a huge crack across it. I told my parents what happened and they said I was dreaming but I know what I heard and I will never forget it.

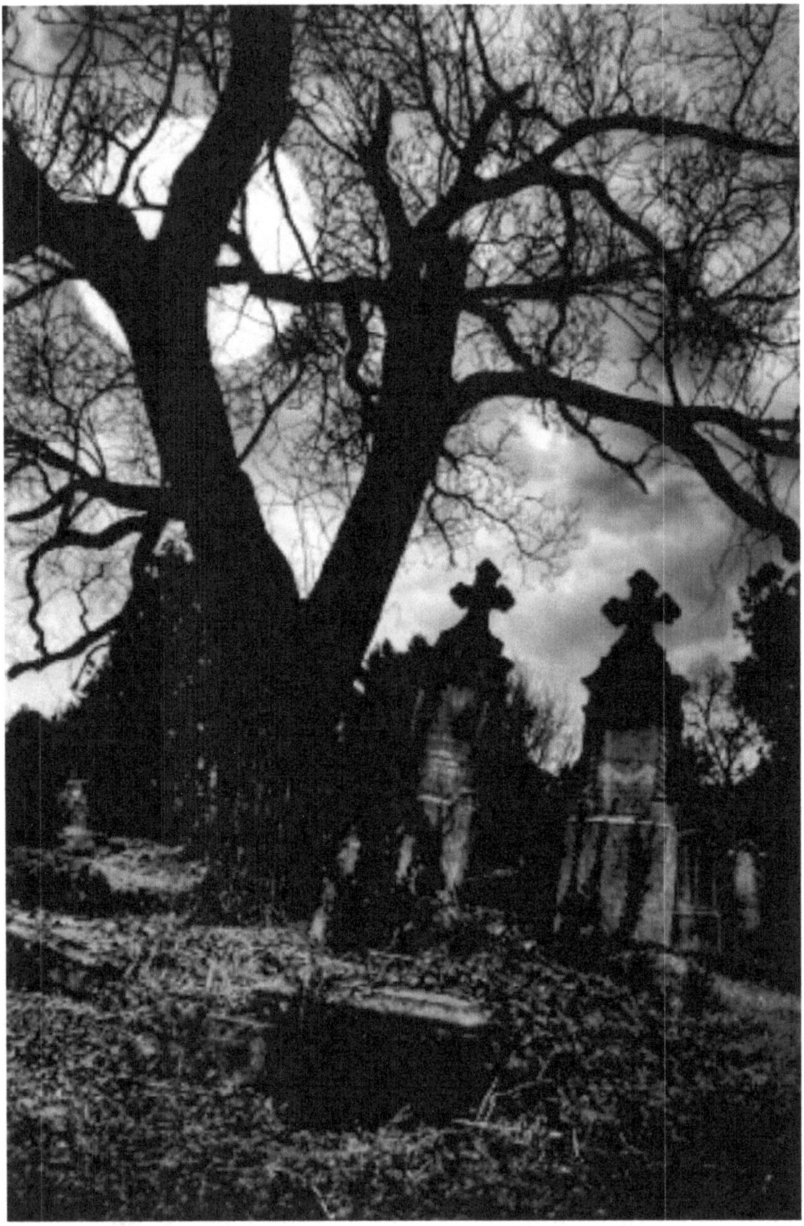

Marbles
Edinburg, Texas

This is a story my mother told me a few years ago that happened to one of her cousins.

When my mother was younger she used to live in Texas and had a lot of family that also lived there. One of her aunts had lived by a cemetery and her cousins would sometimes go and mess around there.

My mom's aunt would tell them to stop messing around, and that they should never take things that were left on the graves.

One of my mom's cousins was at the cemetery one day and had seen some marbles that someone had left on a child's grave, so he took them.

After he came home, he was playing with them for a while and when it was time for bed he left the marbles out in the living room and went to sleep. He was barely drifting off to sleep when he heard the sound of marbles rolling across the floor. He thought maybe it was one his brothers playing with them. He left his room and saw the marbles where he had left them but no one was there. He was getting kind of scared so he put them away and went back to his room to try and get back to sleep, but he heard the noise again. This time he went to his older brother's room to tell him what was happening but his brother was already awake, listening to the marbles rolling on the floor.

When the younger brother told him where he had gotten the marbles from, his brother got angry. While the brothers were talking they could still hear the marbles rolling around. So the older brother went to the living room, grabbed the marbles, went outside and threw them. After that the boys never went back to the cemetery and they never told their mom what happened. ■

Showering Alone?
Lewisville, Texas

One afternoon many years ago when I was around 13 or 14 years old, I had been out playing with some friends on the next street. My parents had made plans for a family dinner. They were going to come home from work and pick up my older brother and me, and we were going to go out to eat.

I had told my friends that I needed to go shower and get ready for dinner with my family (since going out to eat didn't happen often). I came home, said hi to my brother who was watching TV in the living room, and continued on into the bathroom at the end of the hall. I had just finished undressing when I heard something slide across the bathroom door. I quickly turned around and didn't see anything.

I just assumed that my brother was playing with me, so I said, "Very funny!" But, I didn't hear a response.

I brushed off the situation and turned around to turn on

the water for the shower, AND THE KNOB STARTED TURNING ON ITS OWN! I was SOOOOO SCARED! I jumped back and stared at it trying to convince myself that this had really just happened.

During my train of thought the cold water knob had began turning as well. Once it stopped I reached into the water, and it was the PERFECT temperature for my liking. This also creeped me out even more. At that point I grabbed my towel hanging on the hook and ran into the living room and told my brother to please turn the water off for me. He was very stubborn and wouldn't do it because he knew I was capable of doing it myself.

I finally convinced him to go for me once he saw the tears begin to fall from my eyes. After he had turned the water off, he made me tell him what happened. We agreed it best not to tell my parents about what had happened that day, because they are VERY closed-minded people and would have either not believed me or put me in therapy.

So I sat there on the couch for about an hour, in just my towel, trying to shake the thought. I couldn't even go to my room to get clothes, considering my room was not even a foot from the bathroom door. ■

Someone In the Corner
Mission, Texas

When I was younger, I had woken up in the middle of the night. I know I wasn't dreaming because I could feel my skin and I even pinched myself, and it did hurt.

In front of where I was at, in front of the bed, in the corner of the wall, there was the tall person/thing. It was dark and it was just looking at me with those dark eyes. It was carrying something, which looked like some kind of a stick. But, the person or whatever it was too tall, it almost reached to the ceiling. I could tell that it wasn't wearing anything, even though it was so dark, but that thing was straight up skinny. I was REALLY scared.

I just put the blankets over me and hoped I would fall asleep, which I did.

Ten years later, in another house, I woke up in the middle of the night again and after so many years I saw the same thing. Except this time, it was A LOT shorter, shorter than me, and it started walking to me. I was scared out of my pants.

Then all of a sudden when it was just getting really close to me everything stopped.

My best friend had been sleeping next to me, and no, it wasn't her, because she isn't bald and like four feet short and like super skinny like that. That night, she had seen a lady in my room with a dress. I don't know what the heck I saw, but I don't want to see it again. Have you heard of something like this happening to someone like this before?
■

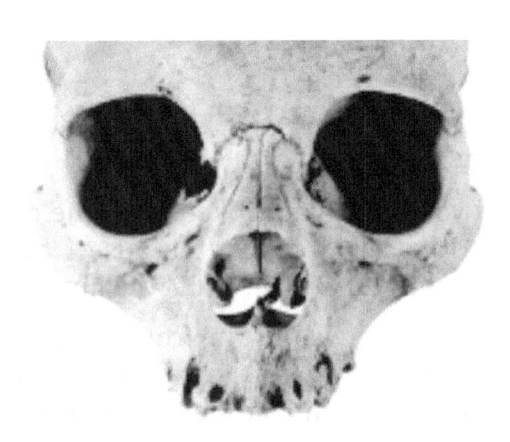

Man On The Couch
Weatherford, Texas

I lived in Texas for five years. From the time I was three until my family moved, my brother and I shared a room. He was a newborn, I'm the oldest.

Where our room was, there was a hallway that lead straight to the the living room. From my room you could see the couch in the living room and you could see the front door.

I never liked to be alone in the house because of the presence that I felt. When I was three, I was lying in my bed and I couldn't sleep. I sat up and there was a figure that had red eyes. It was tall. Its legs were way too long, and it was staring at me. It got really cold in the room.

This took place every day for a year. He was always staring at me. The following year it would begin shoving me out of my bed.

I never knew what it was until I got older. I was watching a ghost show and they described a demon, and for 2 years of my life it was haunting me. My grandpa and grandma bought that place and the last time I went back I saw him again. My grandma moved out and now lives in a new house. And every time I go by the old house, it is always looking at me from the window.

Floating Boy
San Antonio, Texas

It was about 10:00 p.m., sometime in late July. I was spending the night at my friend's house and having a lot of fun. About 11:30 we were getting tired so we tried everything to keep ourselves awake. Nothing seemed to work, so we decided the best way to go about staying awake was to be too scared to go to sleep.

We started to tell each other ghost stories, when all of a sudden we heard a loud crash. We thought it was just my friend's brother, so we blew it off. But, about five minutes later we heard it again.

We started to get angry, so I yelled, "Knock it off, dufus!" to her brother.

He yelled back that he hadn't done anything, but we thought he was lying. About ten minutes later, I saw someone out of the corner of my eye. I assumed it was my friend's brother.

Without turning around to look at him, I said, "Come to confess?"

When I did turn around, I got the shock of my life. There stood (or should I say, floated) a young boy about the age of nine. He was very thin and scraggly, and wore a long, white t-shirt. He just floated there about ten seconds, looking right at us, then disappeared.

I was so scared I could barely move. All I could do was sit

there in awe. Finally, I came back to my senses and screamed. My friend's parents came running in and asked us what was going on. We told them and they told us they had seen him, too. I called my mom to come pick me up and haven't been back to her house since. ◼

Irritated
Dallas, Texas

I am 18 years old and married, and I have a couple of creepy stories. If you didn't notice, the title of this story is "Irritated." Well, I am the one who is irritated, not the ghost.

I have always been a big believer when it comes to the paranormal, and especially so after my grandmother visited me one night about a year after she died. But this isn't about her.

At 17, my husband and I moved into my tiny one-bedroom apartment around Halloween. We had hardly seen any neighbors until we hung up our Halloween decorations that looked like crime scene tape, and that's when we heard the story.

Apparently there was a lady that lived in my apartment who was real crazy. She would walk around the apartment complex with her mother's ashes, talking to herself. Some of the upstairs neighbors even swore up and down that they would hear her scream at night, and then out of nowhere start laughing hysterically. Then she just disappeared.

My husband and I see people or figures passing our bathroom. Our door handles jiggle, and sometimes it turns on our lights and faucets -- things to just really irritate me. It also LOVES scaring our company.

I am getting so annoyed and I keep telling it that it is annoying me, but it won't stop. And I am ready to b-word slap a ghost! What should I do? ■

Deadly Fan
Uvalde, Texas

I know this story is short, but it's weird. In my garage I have 2 ceiling fans. Well one day it was scorching hot, so I turned the fan up to high. With our fan if you touch it while it's on high it will cut the crap out of your finger to where you have to get stitches.

I had it on high when all of a sudden it stops. Our fan is very dusty. Well it stopped, but the other one kept going. I went over to it and touched it, and then it started again. Luckily I jumped back before it hit me. I turned it off and started inspecting it. And I found a large handprint on one of the propellers.

I looked for research on the house and found out a fan had fallen on a man. Looks like he didn't like that particular fan. ■

How Did You Die?
San Angelo, Texas

After my family and I started using the Ouija board weird things would happen, like unexplained noises, and my grandmother seeing a black figure run from the hall into her bedroom.

My family didn't know that after you were done using the Ouija board, you HAVE to say goodbye or the ghost won't know to leave. I wish we knew that. Then maybe none of this would have happened...

When we were using the Ouija board we asked it if there was a spirit in our house. It said YES, and also spelled out a name. Since it was so long ago I don't remember the name ,but I do know it was a guy's name. Anyway with me being very little (6-7) this was all very interesting to me. So I decided to play a little ghost hunter myself.

I invited my friend who lived next door to me to come over when she did I told her what was going on in my house and she decided she wanted to play ghost hunter too. We decided to write a note to this "supposed" spirit asking it questions like, "How old were you when you died?", and "How did you die?". Once we were done we made sure my mom and grandma weren't there. They weren't, as both of their cars were gone. We wanted to make sure nobody that was "LIVING" could write on the letter. So we went into the back room and played for a while. About an hour and a half later we came back and the letter had been written on in handwriting that did not match any of my family members.

There were answers to all of my questions like, "how old were you when you died," etc. Except one question in particular was not answered. The question, "how did you die?" was left unanswered. We wrote many more letters after that, asking many more questions (oh and I don't remember the answer to the how old were you when you died, since it has been a long time now). But, we always asked that same question, "how did you die?" But, it was never, ever answered. I don't understand why that spirit wouldn't answer that question.

Joe Kwon's True Ghost Stories

The Girl In The Doorway
Houston, Texas

It was the summer of 2006 or 2005, I don't really remember for sure. I was about 14 or 15 years old.

I had to go to summer school for this program I was in. The program was being held at another middle school for the summer, so I had to wait for a school bus to pick me up in the mornings. The night before I had to go to school my mother and little sister decided to sleep in the living room, to stay up watching movies.

It was about 7 a.m. and my mother and sister were still asleep on the floor. I was waiting on the couch looking out the window for the school bus. About 15 or 20 minutes went by and yet no bus as I still stared out the window.

Out of complete silence I heard my name being called out, "Sabrina!"

I didn't recognize the voice, and it gave me the creeps and chills. I turned around to see who it was, and standing there in the middle of the kitchen doorway was a girl about the age of ten or twelve.

I tried getting up to wake up my mother, but I could not move or talk. The girl just kept screaming my name with an ugly tone followed by an evil laugh. She was there for about a minute or two until she disappeared and reappeared in front of my parents' bedroom. She just stared at me with the ugliest eyes you could ever imagine.

Within a couple of seconds she disappeared, and I was able to move and talk. I was shocked at what I had just seen and started crying! My mother woke up to my crying and got up quickly and asked me what was wrong. I told her what happened, but I'm not sure if she believed me.

The same night, I was going to sleep in my big sister's room. Something happened... my older sister was just falling asleep, as I was trying to. It was silence once again and out of nowhere I heard the girls voice again but not evil, like if she was in trouble. She asked me to help her.

After she asked me for help, I heard a man laugh in an evil, demonic way. I began to cry.

My sister woke up and hugged me saying everything is going to be okay.

The next couple of days everything went back to normal until my older sister decided to go sleep on the couch. My father was rarely home at night. That night she thought she heard my dad come in the house so she pretended to be asleep. She felt him standing over her so she peeked to see what he was doing. All she saw was a black figure of a hefty man standing there looking down at her, breathing heavy.

Then the figure said "Ya'll are all going to HELL!" and walked away. She thought to herself that my dad might have been drunk, so she ignored him and fell to sleep. In the morning she told my mom what my father did last night. She just looked at my sister confused, telling her that my father called and said he was down the street with his friend Jorge drinking on the porch. They decided to call my father to make sure. He said that he hadn't come home, and that he would be home in a bit.

We were all confused by the strange things that were happening in the house so we decided to ignore it and pretend nothing had ever happened, and nothing more did happen.

Still, to this day I cannot forget how she looked when I saw her standing at the doorway. She had grey/green pale skin, hair down to her shoulders all tangled, eyes that were pitch black, with a big dent or mark on her face (right cheek), wearing an old fashioned white dress with pink polka dots.

Mike's Back
The Woodlands, Texas

This is a story told to me by my mother, which was told to her by my great grandmother as she was dying.

My mother's mother was raised in Hazelton, PA near the Poconos. My Gran's father Mike was a coal miner and an alcoholic. I never heard many good things about him, (he passed away when I was a baby) and my mom said he beat my great granny and the three kids (my Gran, her sister, and her brother).

Shortly after he passed, (I don't remember what he died of), my granny started waking up in the night to hear him calling for her, over and over, in the darkness, though she never saw him.

"Martha! Martha, come with me!" This continued on more than one occasion.

She wasn't afraid, but felt comforted knowing he was still there, even though it made her a little uneasy since he was dead.

Weeks later, a neighbor approached granny (not knowing Mike had died) and said, "I hadn't seen Mike in a while. When did he get back?"

My Grammy was confused and inquired, "When did he get back?"

He replied, "Yeah, I saw him in the backyard the other day. I waved at him but he didn't say hello." At this point my Granny had to tell him why he couldn't have seen him, but the neighbor was absolutely certain that he had. Other people said they saw him looking out the window on more than one occasion, though never smiling.

Two months after Mike started calling for my Granny, she was diagnosed with cancer. She passed away the following year. ■

Henderson Street
Bridgeport, Texas

There have been several ghostly instances in a house on Henderson Street. My parents rented the house during a week when my sister and I were away at North Texas State University for a college summer camp.

When we came back from NTSU, our parents picked us up. But, instead of taking us to our house in Runaway Bay, we stopped at a big green house at the end of Henderson

Street in the middle of town. Our parents told us that this is where we now live.

My temporary room was the dining room when we first moved in. My headboard rested against the sliding doors leading to the living room. The closet, as creepy as that was to begin with, was on the opposite side of this door. I always hated that closet because something was in there watching me.

Anyway, one night I was asleep and all of a sudden I felt four 'hands' pulling me up into the air. I floated past my door and up the stairs to my parents' room. I was frozen and couldn't call out.

When I arrived at the top of the stairs, I managed to finally scream to my mother, "Mom, we have ghosts in this house." At that point I was dropped back onto my bed and awoke with sweat dripping off of every part of my body.

I never inquired about the history of the house because I was too afraid of what I might find out. The haunted areas seem to permeate the house, with the exception of my sister's bedroom. My room was only a small part of the focus.

My parents' bedroom had a very unhappy feeling about it, especially the closet and the bathroom. My mother said that she always had an aversion to the closet same as me.

Their bedroom was located above the garage and I had the same feeling in the garage as I had in their room. When I was told to go up there, I had to pass the closet, and I always did so very reluctantly.

When I was out in the backyard of the house, I always had the feeling that I was being watched from the house.

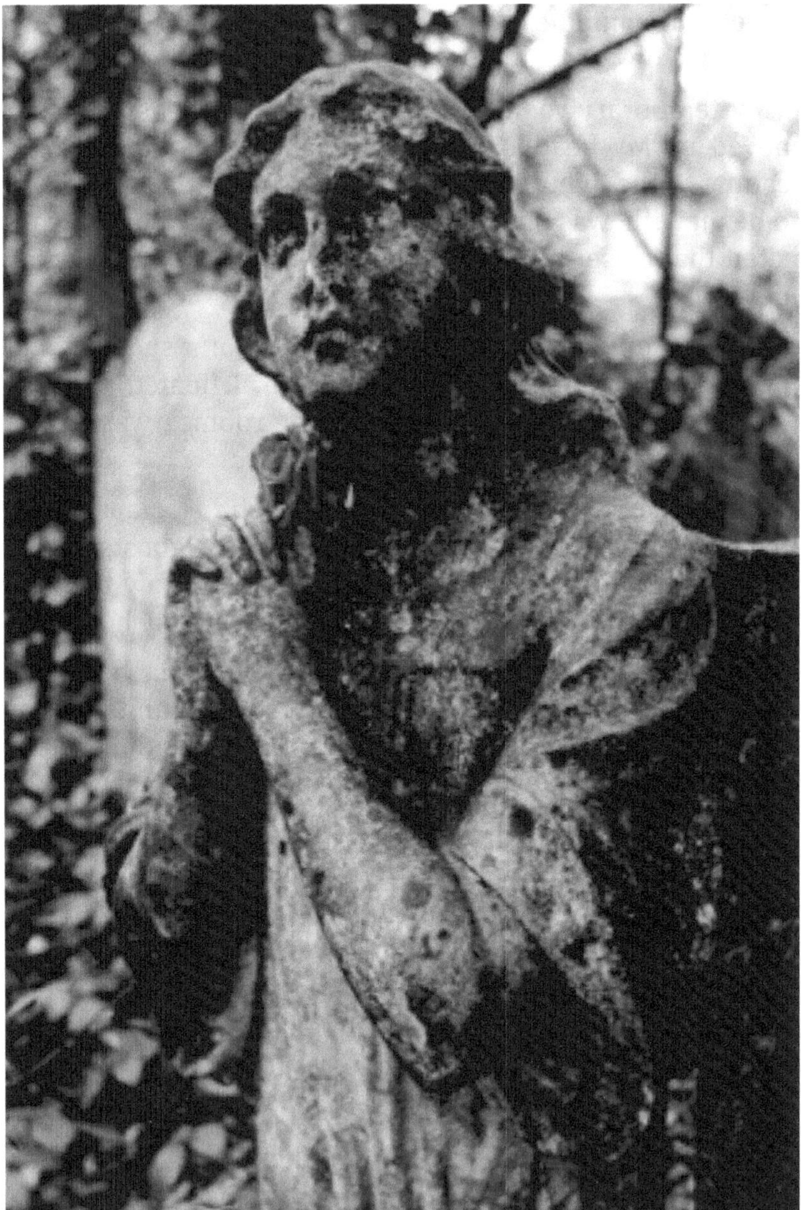

A Visit to the Cemetery
Beaumont, Texas

A few days ago with some friends, I went to a nearby cemetery. A baby sister of one of them had just died, but it hadn't been published. The family ordered that. We were walking on the sidewalk towards the baby area, and I felt something cold rub my shoulder. I looked down and realized we were at my own father's grave. I told them to go ahead, I wanted to spend some time alone.

I was kneeling down by the grave and I suddenly felt that same thing, but on both shoulders. I just stayed there, knowing that if it was a spirit, it was most likely my father. That was something he always did.

Deciding to rejoin them, I went to get up, but it felt like something was sitting on my back.

It was as if this invisible force was trying to hold me down. I was looking around for my friends, but I couldn't see them. And whenever I tried to yell for them, no sound would come out.

I can't remember anything after that, but one of my friends said she was right there the whole time and she saw me fall forward. I have a large knot on my back, and I am still trying to find out what happened.

Any advice or suggestions will help a lot.

Confused and Unexplained
Austin, Texas

I was a total skeptic in ghosts before I came face to face with one. I used to think everyone who believed in them were freaks or weirdos, now I'm sorry I ever thought that.

A couple of months ago, one late summer afternoon bored out of my mind, I could think of nothing better to do than go swimming. My neighborhood had a pool, but it was secluded from the rest of the neighborhood and was just right in front of a forest area. It was not the type of place parents would let their daughter go right before nightfall. So I decided to be sneaky and go without telling them. I hopped on my bike and high tailed it to the pool.

When I finally arrived, no one was there and the place had an empty feeling. Of course I was just happy to finally have something to do. I can't remember all I did but I know at some point as the sun was falling, I was texting some friends and the air got ice cold and the pool lights started to flicker. I was so wrapped up in texting at the time so I didn't take any notice of it.

When I got bored with texting I decided to practice my diving on the diving bored. This is where it got scary for me.

As I hit the water and sunk to the bottom, I felt something grab me and pin me down.

I was so confused and didn't know what to do so I just kicked and fought with all might. It still didn't release me and I was running out of breath, I tried to look around one last time as I felt everything giving in. What I saw sticks to my mind forever.

I saw what looked to be a young man, I couldn't see any eyes and his face seemed sunken in, but right next to him was a woman with the same appearance. Both seemed very transparent. I was now dazed and confused and felt as if everything was growing blurry, I remember I pushed one last time against the both of them, and for a unexplained reason, they let me go. I sprang to the surface and coughed up water and sucked in air all at the same time.

I was tired from all the frantic fighting I had done under water, so my arms and legs were shaking as I climbed out of the pool. I then heard what sounded like a thousand voices say, "Kill, kill, kill."

What confuses me even more, "Jinns will kill."

I'd like to know what a jinn is, and why it wanted to kill me.

Anyway, I pedaled as fast as my shaking legs would pedal, and even then I could still hear the voices ranting, "Jinns will kill!" over and over again.

When I finally made it home my mom and dad were there to scold me for going without permission and comfort me from my terrifying ordeal.

This experience has left me with questions that no one seems to know the answer to. So I ask again, what is a Jinn? Was it what tried to drown me? And if so, why? I have a feeling it is not the actual pool that is haunted, but the woods.

Lewisville High School Ghost
Lewisville, Texas

When I was 16 years old, I was sitting in my last class of the day. It was math class, which I found to be truly my least favorite subject. Needless to say I was day dreaming the time away, thinking of other things, waiting for the time to pass and end my day.

I sat about two rows from the front of the class, directly in the middle. There was a circular clock on the wall just above and directly in the center of the chalkboard. As I glanced up to register the time, 3:15 p.m., I felt a rush of electricity (or something close to it like holding an electrical fence) come from the top of my head flowing down through the bottom of my feet.

As this was occurring, my sight left me, replacing my surroundings with the face of a young girl from the shoulders up. Everything around her was white, with no other images around her. She had at least shoulder length medium brown hair, large oval brown eyes, wore no make up, and had a plain face. Her hair was parted down the middle, like in the 60's-70's style.

With this electrical energy came a surge of information. She told me her she was angry that her life had ended too soon, but that she wanted me to know she was not angry with me. All this seemed to happen in slow motion, but couldn't have taken more than a second.

I came back to reality as quickly as I had left it, sitting back in my chair stunned. I looked around at my classmates, but no one had noticed my reactions.

After this, apparently she took a liking to me and followed me home. My cat was constantly trying to protect me from things I could not see, hissing at the corners of my bedroom at night. I'd hear footsteps outside my bedroom window;

until I would awaken my mother and tell her there was an intruder outside. There never was anyone found upon investigation.

Finally, I awoke suddenly one night and looked at the time. It was 3:15 a.m. I looked to the end of my bed, which was sitting along the same side of the wall my door was on. I had a full-length mirror hanging on my door.

I looked down at the end of my bed to see this girl, standing there staring at her reflection in my mirror with her hands on her hips. As I watched her she turned to look at me and disappeared.

I'm not for sure if the activity ceased after that night, but I moved out of the house and I never saw her after that night. I have come to the conclusion that she must have died in the school, but I do not know how to confirm this.

Any ideas? ■

My New Unwanted Roommate
Lake Jackson, Texas

I have submitted a few stories stating that I am a subtle believer in ghosts, but as of late, that's been changed. My boyfriend and I have been living in the same apartment for two years with no incidents, but now it's different.

Anything that happens, I can almost shrug it off except for a few small details that I cannot explain. It only happens to me, not my boyfriend, which really makes me wonder. I'm the believer in ghosts and he isn't at all, which I think has something to do with these things only happening to me.

One of my experiences happens during the day, every day. I like to keep the blinds on my window open, slatted, not pulled up, but every time I go upstairs, even for just a minute, I come back downstairs to find them tightly closed. I go through the motion of opening them a few times a day before I just give up and let them stay closed.

Another one is at night. I have to keep a rubber stopper in front of my bathroom door or else it will close and the clothes hamper, which is made of metal and does not have wheels, will be pushed right against the door, making it hard to open.

The spare room across from our bedroom is constantly freezing now, and on occasion, the door will slam shut and lock itself.

That door does not close easily because the frame is broken and you have to pull it to close it. I've gotten used to it, as it is not really frightening but more annoying.

And just a few days ago, my neighbor that had moved out a few weeks ago came back to retrieve the last of her things. She had only lived there for a little over a month, so I asked her why she moved out so suddenly. She admitted that she and a few friends had gotten drunk one night and decided to play with an Ouija board and communicated with the spirit of a little girl. She said the spirit started threatening them, so they quit playing and just threw the board out, and over the next few days, strange things started happening, similar to what's happening to me now, but more violent.

Like her hair would be pulled in the shower, DVDs would fly off her shelf at her, and her gas oven would turn on at night, including the burners, after she went to bed.

She said after that, she was so freaked out she broke her lease and moved out and nothing has happened to her since. I guess her ghost moved in with me. ■

Not my Dad
Cibolo, Texas

I was 8 years old, lying in my bed with strep throat. Between the pain in my throat and the heavy wind on our 70-year-old house, I couldn't sleep.

It was very late when I heard the rummaging in the kitchen. I could see into the kitchen through my doorway, and I sat up to see what the noise was.

There was my dad with his back to me, moving papers & loose change around on the table, in his nightly clothes of tighty-whities and socks.

I was about to call him when I went numb; there was a single problem.

In the light from the lamp above the stove and the moon through the window, I could see he had no head. I gasped loudly, but it didn't turn around or acknowledge me in any way.

I hid under my covers, listening to the rummaging on the

table for what felt like hours. I lay motionless until sunrise, afraid to cross the kitchen to my parents' bedroom.

My door stayed shut at night until we moved.

The Bedroom Visitors
Houston, Texas

I will make my first contribution here a combination of my very first experiences with the paranormal.

I grew up in Spokane, Washington. My grandmother raised me. We lived in a typical 1970's home. My bedroom was on the far end of a long hallway and it faced the living room. From my bed I could see down the hall and I could see the back of a comfy chair. Everything else was blocked from my view by a doorway/wall.

I had a great fear of bedtime due to the things that would happen during the night.

On several occasions I would wake up to the "dancing hands" as I called them. They were hands with full-length opera gloves on. They would appear between my bed and the wall. They seemed to have a spotlight on them that made them appear different colors; sometimes pink, sometimes purple and sometime blue.

They would sway in unison and move around, and I've wondered recently if they were communicating in sign language. That would be ironic, because I am in deaf education now.

Of course as a small child I was petrified and would scream out for my grandmother, who would come in and try to put my mind at ease.

This combined with re-occurring instances where I would wake up to billions of fat black ants crawling all over my pillow was pretty traumatic for a 5 year old but the memory that has stayed with me as if it was yesterday is this one.

I was in bed and had been asleep. I woke up with a start, but as strange as it seems I didn't open my eyes. This was not a conscious decision although I still connect "waking up" with opening one's eyes. However that wasn't the case here. As my mind awoke, three things happened simultaneously; first, an audible sound coming from the living room. It sounded like someone rifling through a shopping bag full of tissue paper. In fact I remember thinking that my grandmother must be unpacking a bag. Next, there was an inaudible voice in my head that said, "Do not open your eyes or he will get you," and, with that voice appeared the outline of two red eyes staring at me through my own closed eyes.

I remember lying there totally overcome with fear. Knowing full well that the voice was telling me the truth, but being even more afraid of what I couldn't see beyond my eyelids. The sound continued to get louder and louder until I couldn't control the fear I felt at not knowing what was happening. So, I opened my eyes!

In an instant of opening my eyes I saw a man run full speed and dive from my doorway across my bed. I felt his weight on the bed and I even felt some part of him hit my toes when he landed.

For years I called him a clown because I didn't have any other way of describing him. I still don't, but today some 39 years later, I know he was not a clown.

He had short slicked-back, shiny black hair. His skin was extremely pale and his lips seemed unusually pink or red.

I don't remember much about his lower half but he wore a sports jacket in black and white tweed or black and white plaid. The elbow on the arm facing me had an oval patch.

He didn't say a word and frankly I'm not sure he was aware of my presence.

Of course all of this happened in an instant and was followed by my bloodcurdling scream. My grandmother came in and searched everywhere for "the clown" but he was long gone and he never returned.

His memory has stayed with me my entire life, and I'm sure there was a purpose for his visit. I just have no idea what it was. ■

Forgotten
Allen, Texas

When I was about four years old, I lived in a small, old house with my parents. It was in that old house that I had my first imaginary friend. Oddly enough, his name was "Ghosty."

Ok. No big deal really. Except for a few things...

First, Ghosty, from what my mom tells me, was always concentrated around two basic areas in the house: The bathroom, and my closet.

Second, odd things would happen around the house, like pictures taken out of the frames, sinks being left on. You know, stuff like that.

When I was under suspicion for these things, I would always blame it on Ghosty. I'm not saying that it was my "friend" but you never know. Especially when my parents have no proof, and I hardly remember the truth myself.

Third, My mom, who accepts the idea of paranormal activity remembered once seeing a mean looking old man in my room by the closet. Next to him was an old woman with unclear facial expressions. I don't remember this at all.

A year later, my sister was born. We had to move to a larger house, and Ghosty disappeared.

Several years later, I hardly remember anything about my "imaginary friend." Most of the things I have explained on this story have been what my mom has explained over the years.

Could I have been interacting with a spirit in my home as a young girl, and simply not remember him now? Are things like that even possible? I'm looking for answers. ∎

An Evil Presence
Censored, Texas

My dad was poor as a kid so instead of having his own room and space, he had to share with his other four siblings with only two rooms in the house. So, to have some independence and privacy, he created a bedroom in the separate garage. It had no windows so it was extremely dark at night, but he liked it.

One night in his room he awoke for no reason. He didn't hear a thing, see a thing because it was so dark, smell anything, but he felt some presence. An extremely evil presence.

As he lay awake in his bed pondering on what he should do, he was petrified and didn't want to move, he was so frightened. All he could do is try to hide under his covers.

The presence was so evil it made him sick to his stomach and he felt so small and helpless, alone in the pitch-black garage. He could just imagine the creature or demon approaching him to harm him.

It was such an eerie silence and he couldn't even see his hand six inches away from his face.

The feeling of such an ugly, horrible being grew more and more until he felt so sick and scared he prayed to God even though he was not so religious. He said, "Please help me God, please!" And then all of a sudden the evil presence vanished just as fast as he said those words. He felt such relief and warmth and fell asleep so easily as if he was being cradled by God. ■

Ghost Girl, Are You A Friend?
Snyder, Texas

It started after my 8th birthday. I am 20 now and I've seen her about 40 times since then.

Every time I have seen her she is in a blue summer dress and white socks. She is always very calm but very pale. She always gives me the feeling of despair and discomfort. I always think she is trying to hurt me.

The first time I met her it was midnight and I couldn't sleep. I got up to tell my mom I didn't feel good. Then I saw a flash of blue and heard a giggle. I went into the kitchen and there was this 8 year old girl just standing there watching me. I was completely mortified because I was in my boxer shorts and that was it. I tried to cry out to my mom but the girl did a shushing motion and my cry caught in my throat.

Then I said, "Who are y...y...you?" She smiled, but said nothing.

That's when I got the feeling I was in danger. She smiled again and nodded, as if she was acknowledging my sudden thoughts of danger.

I asked her, "Ghost girl, are you a friend?" She just looked at me and just stood there. I turned to go to my mom's room when suddenly I felt this agonizing pain shoot through my body.

I was so angry with her I turned around and yelled, "Stop!" But, she wasn't there. My mom came into the kitchen and asked what I was yelling stop for, and I told her I must have been sleepwalking.

Since then I have seen her several times and several times I have told her I'm too old, go away. It never really worked but she has never tried to hurt me ever again since the first time I saw her.

She shows up more often, but that first meeting was the most physical she has ever been. She seems to be less corporal as before, but when I am scared or worried she is very corporeal.

So that's my story and there it is like it or not and she never changes except for how physically there she is.

The Good and the Bad
Odessa, Texas

My experiences with a certain ghost began when I was six years old. I had been asleep in my room (in a mobile home) when I woke up because I could feel something watching me. I looked around the room and my closet door was open.

I never shut it before this incident, and I saw something sitting in the corner of the closet. It had moved my clothes on the bar so that they would not hide it. I think it wanted me to see it because it began to laugh at me.

I began screaming and my mother ran into the room but she never saw it.

I didn't have another sighting until I was 9. We had moved to Kermit, TX and I spent most of the afternoons alone until my dad got home from work.

I always felt something around me but nothing ever really happened. I always made sure to shut my closet doors for obvious reasons.

So, when I woke up one night with that feeling I remembered so well, I looked toward my closet and the door was still shut. I rolled over and saw it looking at me from outside my window.

It was not as clear as before and it did not laugh. I rolled over again and told myself that it had to be a dream, but I could not return to sleep and I could feel it was there all night.

This happened on and off for some time. The occurrences did not get really bad until we moved to Monahans, TX when I was 10.

I had gotten to where I could sleep through the presence of the thing, and after a few months of peace (for me at least) I think that it began to get angry.

One night I was asleep on the top bunk of the beds my sister and I shared, when I woke up because something had grabbed my ankles and was trying to pull me off the bed.

I began screaming and my stepmother ran in to help me. I told her what happened. I was crying so much that I don't think she understood much of what I was saying.

She said that it looked as though my ankles were caught in the sheet and she left. I felt like an idiot until I tried to free my ankles and I realized that the sheets had been looped around my ankles and tied in a knot. That's when I knew that it would not let me ignore it.

Now I think it had more confidence because it began to follow me everywhere. Only now it would walk around our house and stare at me from my bedroom door and sometimes it would sit on the edge of the bed while I slept.

It got so common that I really didn't care anymore. Then when I got into high school it came out more often.

I was on my way to the basement of the auditorium with another girl when I was pushed down the stairs. The girl beside me didn't fall and I know she didn't push me because the others would have seen her. I wasn't hurt except for a couple of bruises.

Another time I was walking up the stairs to the stage when I almost fell backwards off of them. Something stopped my fall and held me still until I regained my balance. This was when I started talking to it. It never really answered me. It saved me from several accidents in the auditorium but never failed to knock me down if it was angry.

I think the worst feeling I ever had was when I was early for a meeting at the auditorium and no one else was there. I tried the door to see if it was open and it was. The work lights for the stage were on and I went down to the basement to see if anyone was there. That is when I got the feeling that I needed to run. So I turned around and walked as quickly and calmly as I could to get out of the place. When I got to the front door my teacher was unlocking the door to get in and it was gone.

Those are the worst things that have happened to me but it follows me everywhere and the feelings are always shifting. I wonder sometimes if there are two or just one with wildly swinging feelings toward me. I just wish that I could be alone for a little while in my life. ∎

Normanna's Bridge
Normanna, Texas

Being 18, with a bunch of new friends, in a whole new town, and a new car sounded exciting. The problem was, I lived in Beeville, Texas. There was absolutely NOTHING to do, but cruise or go bowling. I never liked bowling, and cruising got old fast, especially with gas price on the rise.

One night, after watching a ghost video my friend's aunt recorded in her home, we decided to go ghost hunting. I was always a believer in ghosts, and the idea of having a chance at seeing one excited me. After hitting up a few cemeteries and supposed haunted houses, we started to get bored.

Then, a friend of mine shouted, "The Normanna Bridge!"

I never had heard of the bridge, so I was glad to hear about something new. Then, before I knew it, I was following directions on how to get there.

Normanna was about 10 minutes away from Beeville and very easy to miss. It doesn't look like much on the highway, but if you make the right left turn, and you'll see the small town.

It had to have been around 9 p.m. when we got there, and VERY dark. I couldn't see the bridge, but a friend of mine said, "We're here!"

That's when I saw the vine covered, old wooden bridge. It was creepy just looking at it.

I parked around the back, where the bridge was, and saw it was blocked off by a thick, metal rail. My friends and I crossed the bridge, and that's where we all saw red eyes looking right at us from the bushes, below the bridge!

Instinct kicked in, and we all ran to my car. As were trying to climb in all at once, I saw this dim light south of where my car was parked. Then, I realized I was not the only one seeing it.

All I heard was, "Are y'all seeing what I'm seeing?" and, "What the hell is that?!"

I then made out the mysterious light, as a small fire. The fire was not your ordinary flickering, orange, reddish looking fire, but white, with one tall flame right smack in the middle. I had seen it start, and realized that it had started all by itself, and so did the others.

Before I knew it, I was in the backseat of my own car, and

scared out of my mind worse than when we saw the eyes. Red eyes can be explained, (maybe a cat) but a fire starting all by itself, and looking like that, was unnatural, and unexplainable. We drove off, silently. That's when the driver suggested we go back, and see if it was there. All of us agreed. We had not driven very far, not even a block.

As we drove up, there was absolutely no fire. Not one trace of there being one. Come to think about it, the air never filled up with the smell of burning grass, or timber. We just asked ourselves if we had actually saw what we had saw, and just couldn't believe that in just a few seconds that we had drove off, it had completely disappeared!

Then, all of a sudden, there it was. We watched in shock, as the same mysterious fire started taking its form of white, with one flame in the middle. This time, something else in the background was forming out of the same color of white as the flame.

My friend turned the car around, and we all slept in the same room that night. My cousin Erica and I still speak of that night, and wonder what the mysterious flame might've been, but we come up empty handed as far as explanations go.

We've gone back and seen some strange bright lights in the woods behind the bridge, but we've never seen that flame, or the mysterious object around it.

One time, we even heard a man screaming bloody murder, as if it were right next to us, and just a couple of seconds later, a woman screamed the same way.

The woman's scream sounded like it came from the other side of the new bridge they built, right next to the old one. Her scream was this terrified, screeching scream like in horror flicks, and I haven't gone back since.

Some say that slaves were hung on that bridge, and some say a young girl killed herself off that bridge. One thing's for sure, there is something, or someone, unnatural lurking about that place, and I hope someday a crew whom specializes in that criteria, would come and investigate, and see what it could be. Maybe someone is in need of peace, or maybe it's something just downright evil.

The Growling Ghost
Spring, Texas

A few years ago I became very interested in the paranormal and immersed myself in learning about everything from astral travel to energy healing. This ferocious curiosity was a result of some bizarre happenings that lasted approximately a month or more. I'm going to save that story for another time and move forward to 2004, approximately three years later.

My husband and I had been invited by another paranormal enthusiast and her family to a beach home they rented. There were some cemeteries nearby and an abandoned house that had quite a history... so I packed up my camera, digital recorder and sage (my personal method for protection) and headed to Galveston!

The night of investigating was uneventful and we came back to the beach house and headed for bed. My husband as usual went to sleep immediately and I decided to read. Before long I began to feel sleepy, so I placed my book upside down and open on top of my suitcase, which was beside the bed on the floor. Before long I drifted off to sleep.

At some point during the night I awoke to a huge CRASH! I naturally had my heart in my throat but decided that my book must have fallen from the suitcase and I went back to sleep. In retrospect I realize the noise was much too loud to have been a book falling such a short distance but it worked for me at the time.

I was awakened again that night and this time there was no crash... this time I heard growling. Low, deep and gutteral, and it seemed to be coming from under my bed. Now, this is a perfect example of how the human mind attempts to rationalize what it can't understand. I decided the sound was a coming from my friend's tiny Yorkshire terrier. I assumed she'd gotten locked in our room and wasn't happy about it. So, I hopped out of bed and opened the bedroom door to let her out. I called her and made smoochy noises in hopes of coaxing her out from under my bed. However she never made an appearance so I finally gave up and crawled in beside my husband and went to sleep.

The third time "it" woke me up, it was a bit more forceful. This time the bed shook and the growling was even more insistent, and again I thought it was the Yorkie and THIS time she was leaving! I turned on the light and leaned over the side of the bed and began trying to coax the little beast out! Suddenly I realized two things... my book had NOT fallen off of my suitcase and there was no Yorkie under the bed!

My husband finally woke up to find out what was going on. "What are you doing?" he asked sleepily... "Oh there is something growling and shaking the bed and I'm trying to find it!" I replied absentmindedly.

"Hmmm, okayyyyy," he mumbled as he turned over and went back to sleep. (Thanks honey I appreciate your protective nature at times like that.) ■

The Growling Ghost Speaks
Spring, Texas

In my last submission, The Growling Ghost, I shared an experience I had in a beach house and how I spent most of the night trying to locate the cause of several strange noises and the shaking of my bed.

To continue from where I left off, I was finally allowed a few hours of uninterrupted sleep.

My friend woke me right before sunrise to go to the beach and take photos of the ocean. While we were walking I told her about my strange evening. The home belonged to a friend of hers and as far as she knew there had never been anything paranormal occurring there... BUT maybe we had brought something back from one of our investigation sites the night before! We decided to investigate the house before we packed up and left.

When we got back to the house I got my digital recorder set up and began taking photos around the bedroom. My daughter, who thinks my hobby is "stupid and a waste of time", came into the room and plopped on the foot of the bed.

She sat for a couple of minutes and suddenly, like a shot, she jumped off of the bed and headed for the door. "What's wrong?" I inquired to her fast-retreating backside.

"The bed shook!" she stammered from the safety of the living room.

We continued to investigate, and eventually burned some

incense and tried to cleanse the space of any negativity.

So, that was that! We packed up and headed back to Houston. On the way home I put my ear buds in and began to listen to the digital recordings we took. There wasn't anything to speak of until my daughter entered the room. Right before she bolted for the door there was a break in the recording and as clear as day a hoarse voice whispered "Priya," my daughter's name! (Pronounced Preeya.) This is an unusual name and very easy to recognize. Then you hear Priya make her hasty retreat!

I was so shocked by what I heard that I passed it back to my daughter and just said, "Listen and tell me what you hear!" A few seconds later she looked up at me and said, "It said my name!"

That EVP hit a little too close to home and I haven't been able to listen to my EVPs with the same feeling of security nor have I been as involved in the investigation aspect of the paranormal. ■

Unknown Bruises
Killeen, Texas

I am not sure where to begin. All I know is I could be in trouble and need help regarding the unexplained.

It started a few weeks ago. I began having dreams, very dark dreams. At first it was a shadow in my room, in the corner that would watch me sleep. Then a week ago the shadow began to breathe on me. I couldn't scream or move. Reading stories and other comments on here, I began to think it was sleep paralysis. But then I began to dream the shadow would grab me, I could feel it grab my leg, then one night the muscles in my back. The scary thing is, every place I dream I've been touched by it, I find a bruise.

I wake up remembering the dream and now I look for marks. I wake up in a cold sweat, which is why I know I am sleeping when it occurs.

The shadow is obsessed with me. It now grabs me several times throughout the week. ■

Unknown Bruises Update
Killeen, Texas

I am starting to get scared, very scared. Last night the dark figure grabbed me again, it again left a bruise but this time the bruise is in the shape of a heart. I have done some research and it most likely is a demon. However it happens in my dreams, I know I am not awake when it occurs because I again wake up in a cold sweat. I really need help, should I call a priest?

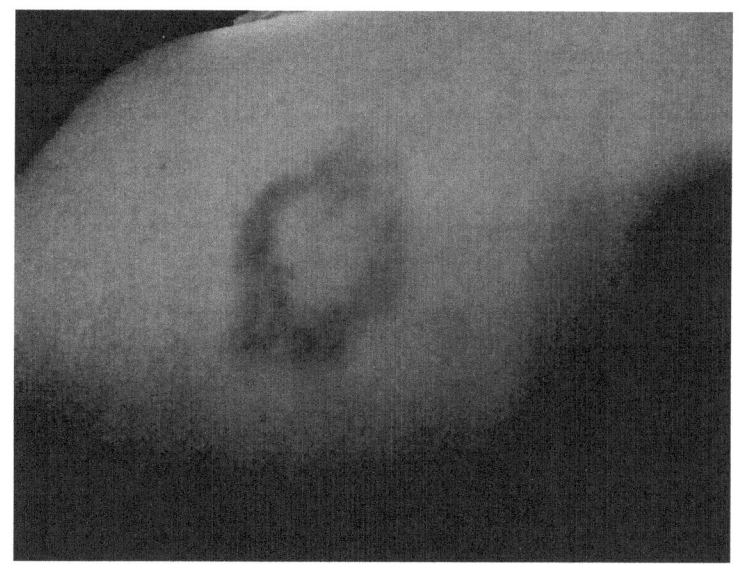

Was That A Ghost?
Dallas, Texas

I have had many experiences with the paranormal. This happened when I was just 5-6 years old. One Halloween, I was looking through my candy and everything went black. When I recovered, my candy was thrown everywhere, my costume was torn to shreds, and my brother was in the fetal position in the corner. But this is not the reason why I'm writing this. Here is the story:

One afternoon I was playing my Nintendo 64. I heard this weird noise coming from the bathroom. It sounded like water being splashed, like someone was being drowned or a child was playing. When I walked into the bathroom, I felt this cold rush go through my body. Being 5 or 6, I was pretty scared. So I went crying to my mom and she said, "It was just the wind, babe."

Later that night, I was cuddling with my Barney. I heard this weird 'meow'. I knew we didn't own cats, so don't know what it was. I looked around the room and on the wall next to me was a shadow of a cat! It played on the wall, rolling over and jumping. I was so scared!

I tried to sleep but every time I tried to sleep it would growl and hiss. I finally managed to sleep. After that it hasn't happened again until last night... I woke up sweating, and on the mirror in a shadow was that cat! ∎

Maybe They Celebrate an Arrival?
Tomball, Texas

I am a teacher in Texas. I went to college and was raised Catholic in a great family. I am the youngest of four and I am 100% normal! I have two little kids and a super awesome husband. I have never experienced anything unusual in my whole life. I have never had to deal with the death of a family member and never really had to attend a funeral of a loved one. I have had a curiosity of the afterlife but have never had a desire to have an experience.

With that being said, that changed on April 23, 2006.

My husband and I dated a long time before we got married. We were both in college and enjoyed spending time with each other's family.

We settled down in Tomball just outside of Houston. His family was in San Antonio. We had our first child in 2003. His mother absolutely loved her. She was her first grandchild and she called her "Pinga".

We made a lot of trips to San Antonio. I loved to spend time with my mother-in-law. She was a wonderful person. The last time we were there she was not doing so well. I spent spring break with her. I created a beautiful garden in her front yard so she could enjoy the new spring flowers. She was very depressed. She and my father-in-law were having problems. When we drove away I could see her crying in the driveway and my heart sank.

We would talk often. She was very sad. One Friday night she called. My husband was putting our child to bed. She said not to bother him, that she would talk another time with him.

We were busy Saturday and I remember telling my husband that he needed to call his mom. The evening got away from us and it was too late to call her. That night, as I tried to go to sleep, I heard what sounded like a small party. It was so close to where it sounded like it was downstairs. When I lifted my head to hear exactly where it was coming from it stopped. I could hear it when I laid my head down and as soon as I lifted it, it was gone. I woke my husband up and asked him to listen. Nothing. I told him there were people talking and music playing. He listened for a while then went back to sleep.

I laid there for what seemed an eternity. I could hear voices, but couldn't make out their words. I could hear the beat of the music but could not make out the song! We had grilled and ate dinner in the backyard and there were no neighbors out, so what was this? I listened until I fell asleep.

The next day my husband played golf with a coworker while I had lunch with his wife. While talking at the table a young man approached our table and said that my child was precious. He handed me a bracelet that had small colorful crosses around it. He then left. I didn't think it was strange. I thought it was very kind that he gave her this bracelet. I was in mid-sentence talking about my mother-in-law as this happened.

Later that afternoon, I noticed that I had missed many calls from my sister-in-law and her father. When I called her she was at the airport in Dallas waiting to fly to San Antonio. There had been an accident and her Tia (aunt) was in the ICU and they could not find her mom. I ran to my husband and told him to call his dad.

Olga and Becky were passengers in a car that was hit on Highway 281 and Summerglen. The force was so strong that it sent the car off the highway and into the woods. They had been with a friend and his brother at an early mass and he was taking them to his home to see it. He turned into oncoming traffic for some reason.

As we drove to San Antonio, we got a call from his father that his Tia had died. My heart broke to hear my husband quietly cry.

We learned that Olga was talking to a few teachers at her school Friday morning and told one that she was ready to see her mom. She told another that she wondered if she was good enough to go to Heaven.

I believe that what I heard were late relatives celebrating that Olga and Becky were coming and the young man at the restaurant was an angel. The accident happened at 2:13 in the afternoon. The same time I was talking about her at the restaurant. Later my husband said that while they were golfing, the most soothing wind blew and he said that as it blew it made the trees sway back and forth in slow motion. All he and his friend could do was stare.

It will be four years since we lost Olga and Becky. There have been unique incidences that have occurred. They do not scare me. I know that they are trying to let us know that they are with us, and not missing a thing!

Last December, I woke my husband up and asked him if he could hear the men talking in our backyard. I was so scared to think this was a repeat of that one Saturday night in 2006. Same thing - when I lifted my head, nothing, when I laid it down- well, I could hear them but could not make out their words. It sounded like a group of men enjoying one another's company right outside my window.

I got a call the next day that my sister-in-law's father (my husband's brother's wife's father) was killed in a car accident.

I don't believe I have a gift. I just really listen.

Touched
Uvalde, Texas

I'm originally from Houston and recently moved to Uvalde for a new job. I moved into a new apartment with a roommate who would be starting the same day I would. Well my friend was originally from New Jersey and would go home on weekends to visit his family. We had been working our new job for about two months when my roommate decided to go home for a four-day weekend. For most of that weekend I spent just hanging out with my good friend Guz (pronounced Goose), and got home early. I got sleepy and went to sleep around ten.

The first thing I remember about this night is that I was dreaming and woke up because I felt a presence standing next to me. The first thing that went through my head was that one of those crazies must have gotten in and if this gets ugly, I might have to put some hands on him!

At that very moment a hand brushed my cheek. I knew nothing was there; my eyes were already adjusting to the darkness.

I was a bit freaked out, but sleepy too. So, I brushed it off and told myself I'd make sense of it in the morning.

I woke up again, this time I felt like I was paralyzed. I couldn't move and felt a pressure on my chest. I was in shock at what was happening. I was able to look at my chest because my head was on a pillow and I forced myself to look at the area where I felt the pressure. It felt like what ever the pressure was trying to get inside me. When I looked at my chest I could see a blurry mass on top of me. At that moment I did what anyone else would do. I asked the man upstairs for help. At that exact moment I was let go and was able to get up and turn on the lights. I looked at my digital watch that I would keep under my pillow. It was three o'clock. I called Guz and told him what had just happened. He told me he thought it was best I spend the night at his place. I told him that even though I was freaked out a little, I would stay. I didn't want it to think I was scared. So I went to sleep and stuck it out. I kept the lights on. ■

Don't Fear the Reaper
Borger, Texas

My parents were divorced and Daddy lived in Borger, Texas. When I was 13 and would spend the summers with there with my brother. He had a mobile home. My room was in the middle, my brother's room was at the back end, and there was a bathroom in between our rooms.

Daddy was always working and came in very late. My brother was working at a Mexican restaurant. I was home alone on the 4th of July. It was dark, and I didn't have any fireworks, so I stood in the hall window and watched the boys across the alley pop theirs.

My bedroom door was behind me, and my brother's room was to the left of me. I loved to listen to Blue Oyster Cult, Don't fear the Reaper was the one song that I had liked the most. I went in his room to play that song. The second that song started, my bedroom door and the bathroom door both slammed shut at the same time very hard. I blacked out!

I came to when my brother hollered my name. He said that I was sitting in the corner of his bed with the Bible to my chest, frozen. To this day I have no idea how long I was in a trance. We found out not long after that, that the girl my brother was dating worshipped the devil. She got the boot!

Daddy sold the trailer years later. He still stays there, about a week out of every month, in a camper. Lots of things went on, but that was the only thing that happened to me.

My brother is the one that saw and had the most experiences. There is a small town right outside of Borger called Plemons. Charles Manson's clan was there.

Ever heard of Helter Skelter? He intends to go back there when he gets out of prison. An oil Company bought all of the land that Plemons is on, then took the town down, but the spirits still remain. That is where that old girlfriend of my brother would go.

Creepy huh? It's the truth, though. ■

Haunted House
Houston, Texas

My husband, our ten-year old daughter, and I moved into a new house in 1979. Several strange things happened during the 18 years we lived there. My daughter would hear someone knocking on her bedroom door when I would be downstairs in my bedroom with the door closed watching TV. She would hear me calling her name when I wasn't even home.

Frequently, when my sister (same age as my daughter) would spend the night and my husband and I would be out for the evening, they would hear voices, and various noises that scared them to death.

I was home alone one night watching TV with my bedroom door closed, and saw a black shadow moving across the wall in my dressing area.

I was so frightened that I jumped out my window and ran to the neighbor's house.

The police came and searched but nothing unusual was found.

My mother stayed with us for a while and slept in the upstairs bedroom where my daughter used to sleep. She said that one night after she went to bed and had turned the lights out that it felt like someone had laid down on the bed beside her. She actually felt the pressure of the bed moving. She slept with the lights on and went home right afterwards.

Another incident occurred during a Christmas party after everyone had gone home. My father had fallen asleep on the living room sofa. I went to check on him and found him asleep with his mouth open. His lips were not moving, but words were coming from his mouth. He kept saying over and over (but NOT in HIS voice, it was a strange, tiny voice) help me, please help me, help me... I ran to get my mother and husband and we had enough snap to record this phenomenon. It was so scary that we woke him up and told him what was going on. He thought we were crazy until we played the tape back for him. Unfortunately, that tape has disappeared.

My husband never believed in things that go bump in the night, but one morning as he was shaving in the bathroom, he said that while looking in the bathroom mirror, all of a sudden it was not his face looking back at him.

That scared him of course.

Many more strange things happened in that house. My

family was always afraid in that house. We no longer live there. ■

Someone Else...
San Antonio, Texas

This story takes place a long time ago at my grandma's house.

A bunch of my friends and I were playing outside when we decided to play Hide and Go Seek. There were a lot of us so we decided to have two people find everyone else.

We played in a big field that was between my grandma's house and the neighbor's house.

My best friend and I were looking for everyone and across the field we saw a white figure that looked like a kid run behind a rock and hide.

We both laughed and started running towards the rock. We reached the rock I yelled, "Found you!" But there was no one there.

My friend and I got really freaked out, and yelled for everyone to come out of their hiding spots. We asked them who hid behind the rock and they all said no one.

When I saw them come out from their hiding spots, they were all hiding on the opposite side of the field, so I believed them.

We kept playing, but for the rest of the night we never saw the white figure anymore. However, my friend and I are still really freaked out by what happened. ■

Ghost at The Foot of My Bed
Houston, Texas

So this all happened a couple years ago. My niece was about 7. She was accidentally shot by her little brother when they were playing with guns. When her little brother pulled the trigger, he didn't realize the gun was loaded and he shot her in the head and it killed her. Devastating...

So a few nights after she died, I randomly woke up in the middle of the night to find the Disney Channel was on my TV, and I don't go to sleep with the TV on. I then looked down at the end of my bed and saw a young girl watching the TV. I just thought it was my daughter, about 8 years old at the time. So, I didn't think anything of it. I just shut my eyes and tried to go back to sleep. Then for some reason, I opened my eyes a few seconds later and looked to my side and there was my daughter asleep! So at the foot of my bed was NOT my daughter, so I watched the little girl, and all of a sudden she quickly stood up vanished at the doorway.

I strongly believe it was my niece's ghost. ■

Blink
Houston, Texas

When I was just a little boy of about 6 years old, I experienced something very weird.

I was in my room at about 8:30 at night. It was already time for me to go to bed but I was not tired. I decided to stand by my window and listen to the frogs and the crickets as I waited for sleepiness to come. After a good 3 minutes of standing there, something odd happened instantaneously. I blinked, and when I opened my eyes, it was 9:30 in the morning. The sun was out and people were walking their dogs outside. It was Saturday so my parents were not up yet. I was still standing by my window, and I had not fallen asleep. It was as if 13 hours had never even happened, because I was not fatigued from standing, and my legs were still good for another 10 minute standing.

I have no idea how this happened, and I still occasionally look at my clock to find it a different time than it should be, but not on such a large scale as that.

If anyone has any insight on this phenomenon, or if similar has happened to you before, please let me know. This really is not meant as a scary story, simply to get some closure. I do suspect that a spiritual entity is involved, for I have had contact with "them" for many years in my life. Please post a comment if you have an idea of what happened, and if you were expecting a scarier story, I may post some more of my experiences.

Ghost Handprints?
Dallas, Texas

I'm changing names so that way the people I'm talking about in my story will be protected.

It was a breezy May evening, and there was a full moon out. My friend Nicole and I were driving down the road because we were leaving a party. We were just about to cross the railroad that was supposedly to be haunted.

The legend was about a bus full of children who were going across the railroad when an oncoming freight train hit the bus and everyone was killed. Now the ghosts of the young children are haunting the tracks and protecting everyone from danger.

Back to the story:

Not wanting to repeat the crash, I stepped on the gas pedal trying to get safely across, but my car wouldn't cooperate. It suddenly stopped running and we were dead center of the railroad tracks.

Now this started to scare us, but what scared us half to death was that the railroad signals started flashing and two headlights appeared down the track. Panicking, I tried turning to key and hitting the gas pedal trying to get the car started.

"Hurry up Jamie! The train is coming!", Nicole shrieked. The train whistle started blowing, trying to give us a warning to get out of the way.

"We have to get out!", I shouted, reaching for the door handle.

"I can't!", Nicole cried, struggling with the seat belt. Sometimes it wouldn't budge.

I threw myself over to her, trying to undo the seat belt. My hands were trembling and sweat started going down my face.

I could hear the oncoming train. It was getting closer. I glanced over my shoulder to see how far away the train was. It was closer, and you could see the engineer. He was trying to stop and he was whistling loudly trying to get us out of the way.

All of a sudden, out of nowhere, the car was given a hard shove from behind. Nicole and I gasped, and I fell on her lap as the car started to roll forward, slowly at first, but then full speed, and then it stopped. The car cleared the tracks, and two seconds later, the oncoming train roared passed. As the car finally stopped, you could see the engineer waving a fist, and shouting a few curse words because we gave him a fright.

"That was close. But how did you get the car to move?" Nicole asked, both of us shaking badly.

"I didn't. Someone must have helped us.", I said.

I got out of the car and ran to the tracks to thank the person for saving us. You could mostly see everything, because the moonlight penetrated throughout the darkness all around. For about five minutes I searched the area but found no one. I called out a few times but no one answered.

"Where is he?" Nicole asked. She finally freed herself and I guess I didn't hear her come next to me because I jumped.

I shrugged. "No one is here.", I answered her question, puzzled.

"Well maybe he's just shy," she said. "Thank you whoever you are."

Just then, a slight breeze picked up, swirling around us, patting our hair and shoulders, it felt like a child's hand. I shivered and hugged my best friend. We almost died that night, and I'm grateful to be alive.

"Yes, thanks." I whispered.

We went back to the car and I pulled up my cell phone, to call a tow truck. Beside me, Nicole was wide-eyed and speechless, staring at the back of my car.

"Jamie, look!" she gasped.

I stared at the vehicle. Scattered around the back of the car were several glowing handprints... small handprints. They were the size of a seven-year-old. I started trembling again, and then it hit me. Those were the handprints of the children who died in the school bus. They pushed our car out of the way to protect us.

The wind picked up again and this time I heard a faint echo. It sounded like it said "you're welcome" and it patted our shoulders and arms. Then it died down and the handprints faded from the back of the car.

Nicole and I clung together for a moment in terror and delight. A couple minutes later, we let go of each other and I called a local tow truck that came and towed us home. ■

My Sister's Closet
Katy, Texas

One day our only key was locked inside our house so we called my oldest daughter Anna and she let us stay the night at her apartment. She lives with her boyfriend, so it's a very small apartment and we had 6 people staying there that night. I slept in their room with my husband and 3 kids. Her bed faces the closet.

I was awakened that night by rustling in the closet. It sounded as if someone going through clothes. I thought it was my daughter so I ignored it and fell back asleep.

About two hours later I was awakened again. It was about 3:00 a.m. when this was happening. I thought to myself, "What are they doing up so late?" But, I didn't go back to sleep this time.

I looked at the closet and the door was open. I knew for a fact I had closed it because my daughter believed in a monster in the closet.

What I saw made me believe in it too.

There was a shorter person, very muscular with blonde hair and blue eyes. He was standing in the closet a little hunched over and staring straight at me with piercing red eyes.

I couldn't look away. All I did was stare straight back at him.

The next morning I told my husband what had happened. He doesn't believe in the paranormal, so he just said, "Your crazy," and walked away.

I told my oldest daughter and her boyfriend and they had seen it, too. They want to move out, but they can't afford to break their lease. ∎

Red Eyes
La Porte, Texas

This is a story that my grandfather had told me that had happened to him when he was a teenager. You see when my grandpa was younger both of his parents died. So my grandpa and his younger brother had to live with their uncle who treated them badly. For example his uncle would make my grandpa and his brother sit on the back porch and make them wait until his uncle and wife and their kids would eat dinner first, and when they were done they would let my grandpa and his brother come in and eat whatever what was left on the plates.

When my grandpa and his brother got older, his uncle moved them out to this shed-like structure in the back yard. One night my grandpa was walking home and when he reached the shed he walked in and sat on the mattress he had on the floor. There was no door on the shed so he sat looking out where the door used to be waiting for his brother to come home.

He had a small fan on because it was a hot summer's night when all of a sudden he felt like something had blocked the air from coming through. When he started to turn his head to see what it was, all of a sudden this monster-like creature jumped on his back and sank its claws into his shoulders.

My grandpa was frozen and couldn't move. He could feel the thing breathing down his neck and growling in his ear.

My grandpa said all he could think about was his little brother and what would happen when he got home. Would it attack him? Or would it kill my grandpa and let his brother come home and find the last member of his family dead? So, my grandpa said he worked up the courage and managed to get free from the clutches of the monster. As he ran from the shed, he turned back to see if the monster was following him, but it wasn't. All he saw were two big red eyes looking straight at him.

Luckily my grandpa ran into his brother on the road and told him what happened. That was the last time they set foot in that shed, and the last time he saw his uncle.

But not knowing what it was that attacked him was always on his mind.

My Dark Man
Houston, Texas

I first met the dark man when I was about five years old. He first appeared to me in a dream accompanied by two huge black dogs. In the dream he was dressed as a farmer and was using the dogs to hunt me. I awoke from the dream crying and calling for my mom (my dad was out of town) and to my horror I could see the dogs in my room. Upon seeing the dogs I began to scream and my mom came running into my room. She turned on the light and assured me nothing was there but as soon as she turned the lights off the dogs would return.

Finally after turning the lights on and off a few times, my mom took me into bed with her. Though I was now in a different room the dogs still showed up as soon as the lights were out and in addition I could also see the man standing in the hallway. My mom finally left the TV on so I could go to sleep.

I am now 28 years old and the man still watches me. The dogs no longer appear, though they stayed with me well into my teenage years. I don't know who this man is but he still terrifies me to this day. ■

My Dark Man Part 2
Houston, Texas

First off I would like to thank those of you who read my first story. I have decided before I go into some of my later encounters with the man I should describe my early ones.

In the beginning, his best tools in his arsenal of fear were the dogs. As I said before he would always come with two huge black dogs.

I couldn't tell you any specific breed because they didn't seem to have one and they didn't have glowing red eyes or anything like that, but they did smile. As they would advance on my bed, they would smile the most evil grins full of very sharp very white teeth.

The man would always stand towards the back of the room either in shadow or with his face obscured with a wide brimmed hat. As for a description all I can really say for sure is he is tall and thin.

Though I couldn't see his face I could feel his emotion. As my terror of the dogs grew, he seemed more and more pleased. I could feel dark satisfaction radiating off him as my fear increased.

It has always felt to me that he is trying to wear me down and weaken my resolve against him so he can claim me as his own.

When the dogs began to scare me less he quit bringing them and for a while I thought I was safe but he found me again.

My Dark Man Part 3
Houston, Texas

In order to tell my next story I have to give you a little more background on myself. I have been able to see and sense things for as long as I remember, and in December of 2003 I had a strong sense that something was wrong.

I was going to college at the time in San Antonio, and for some reason I couldn't bring myself to sign up for spring courses. My parents kept asking me why I hadn't signed up and all I could tell them is I felt that I wouldn't be able to go.

On December 29, 2003, my father passed away of heart problems. He was only 39 and it came as quite a shock to my family. At that time I was 22, my sister was 18 and my brother 12.

It goes without saying that this was a horrible time for my family. I began having dreams of my father. In some of these my father and I would just talk and I would wake crying but I knew that it was his way of communicating with me and letting me know he was ok.

Then I began having different dreams. My father was still in them, but somehow I knew it wasn't really him it was actually the dark man.

I dreamed that I was out shopping with my mom and a man that looked just like my father approached us. My mom was so happy to see him and hugged him tightly. The man then turned to me and held out his arms to me I recoiled in horror.

This man looked just like my father, he was even wearing my dad's uniform (my dad was active duty air force), but I could tell it wasn't him because of his eyes.

There was coldness in the eyes in front of me that I never saw in my father's. My blood ran cold. I knew that look. I tried to get away from him and he kept telling me that he was my father and he wasn't dead, if I would only come to him, I would see that.

I finally stopped and faced the man, and told him I knew who he truly was. The figure then looked at me and laughed and disappeared. I awoke in a cold sweat and looked around my room. I couldn't see the man anywhere, but I could feel him.

I wish I could say this was the last of his torment, but he would again soon find his way back to me. ■

Axe Me If I Care
Houston, Texas

This is a confession. One I've never spoken of before. Mainly because I never realized the impact of what I've done until just recently. I'm still kind of in disbelief, mostly that I didn't realize there would be repercussions.

I'm going to state something very profound: I'm an axe murderer, and I didn't even know it. Not in the sense that I took an axe and hacked someone into pieces. Not exactly, anyway. But, then again, pretty much sort of. And I'm starting to feel sorry about it I think. It hasn't quite sunk in yet, but I can feel it starting to. I'm just trying to connect with my feelings about this. I'm not sure how I feel about it yet, or how I'm even supposed to feel. Awful, I think. Or maybe I feel awful that I don't feel awful, if that makes any sense.

I was 18 years old and lived with my brother and his two

daughters. They were like sisters to me. Well, ONE was like a sister to me. The younger niece, however, I found to be just a bit of a nuisance. She was "different". Honestly, I saw her as more of an object than a person. I feel like I can see inside of most people, as if I can sense their souls. With her, though, she just seemed empty to me. Just a temporary object in space and time that had no real purpose, no real meaning, no importance at all. And no soul. She was no different to me than a table or a chair, except that she was a nuisance.

One morning I'd gotten up very early (5a.m. or so) when my brother left for work. I had a reason, though. I woke up the older niece and we sneaked into her younger sister's room with the intention of doing something mean to her before she woke up. I don't even remember what we were about to do, but I'm certain it wasn't very nice. Anyway, she woke up and caught us both there beside her bed just as we were about to do it. She asked what we were doing in her room, and she seemed pretty angry. I remember because she started to raise her voice and we didn't want to get in trouble (her mom was still home and sleeping just in the next room). So, I told her she needed to be quiet. But, she didn't take me seriously; so then I had to back that up. I put my hand over her mouth and held it tight across her lips and her jaw. Again I told her in a very quiet, but firm voice, "Shut up!"

The situation was escalating, and I needed to do something fast. In that very instant, a thought came to me, and I spoke it. "The neighbor... the one that lives behind us... Bart... you know, the guy in Alcoholics Anonymous? He's gone crazy. He started drinking again and he's completely drunk and insane... he's got an axe and he's downstairs right now! You HAVE TO BE QUIET!" (Yes, his name really was Bart. We called him "Black Bart" just for fun).

She stopped struggling and her face went soft. I uncovered her mouth and glanced at her older sister. "We're going downstairs to see if he's gone yet. Stay here until we get back," I whispered.

Thinking nothing of this myself, I quietly lead her older sister out of the room. We went straight downstairs to watch television. I assumed she'd fall back to sleep up there and think it was a dream. It never even crossed my mind that she might continue to react after we left her alone in her room. You've heard the term, "out of sight, out of mind"... that's exactly what this was. I never even gave it another thought all morning.

Around noon (nearly 7 hours later) my brother's wife came downstairs. She was madder than a wet hornet. She'd just gotten out of bed and discovered her youngest daughter in a certain state and shaking on the floor in a corner of her room. Unfortunately she'd managed to mumble enough, even in her condition, to get me into deep trouble. My brother was called and he immediately came home from work. It was a rough day for everyone. My brother and his wife admitted that their youngest daughter was "different", but stated it was no excuse to do that to her. Whatever. Except, it seemed to have pushed her over the edge. She'd been up there for hours, cringing in the corner. In her mind, thanks to me, there was a real-live axe murderer downstairs hacking up her family into pieces... and that she could be next. I have to assume this wasn't what made her the way she was, it just happened to be the last straw. She was institutionalized shortly afterward. She ended up killing herself approximately two years later, just shortly after moving back home to her parents' house.

The weekend of the funeral I stayed a night at my brother's house, and slept in the very same upstairs room I'd had as a teenager. It brought back a LOT of memories. While there, I couldn't help but step into my younger niece's old bedroom. And for the first time ever, it felt to me like she was actually present... as if something about her truly existed and was present at that very moment. I never felt that with her while she was alive. Alive, she felt to me as if she were nothing more than an object. This wasn't a creepy feeling; it was simply an unusual feeling. I didn't care if she had a spirit that returned. Not then, anyway. That was 30 years ago.

Two weeks ago I returned to my brother's house for a short visit. I pretty much wasn't allowed back until now, so it was the first time since the funeral that I'd been back there. I again stayed in my old upstairs bedroom, and again I stepped into my deceased niece's room for a moment. The room was uncomfortably cold. I stepped out into the hallway and closed the door behind me. Across the hall I got into bed and quickly fell asleep. During the night I was awakened by a long, low-pitched crying sound. I strained to listen. It continued. I got up and moved to the doorway. The crying continued. I was certain it was coming from my dead niece's room. I immediately assumed it was the older niece in there crying about her younger sister being dead (even after all these years. She kind of feels guilty, too.) So, I went to comfort her. But, opening the door, I found nobody there. There was just enough moonlight coming in through the window on the opposite wall that I could see where I was going. I walked around to the other side of the bed and stood in front of the window. But, there, on the floor, wide-eyed and shaking in the corner was my dead niece. She looked up at me, and seemed to be screaming frantically although there was no sound coming from her. Actually, I don't remember ANY sounds whatsoever once I entered the room. Then she just vanished. I hurried out.

Now it seems to me that it just may be that the spirit of my niece has, perhaps for the last 30 years, been continuously reliving that ordeal I placed upon her. The axe murderer in the house, hunting each of us down one by one, had, to her, been a frightening reality. One that resulted in her death, even if indirectly. I put that reality in her feeble mind, am I responsible for her death? More than that, though, am I responsible for 30 years of her continuous torment even after she's long been dead? I don't know yet what to make of that possibility, nor if I'm even ready to acknowledge this at all. Why does this have to happen to me?

Children of the Railroad
San Antonio, Texas

This story is completely true and bizarre. You can even research it for yourselves.

Years ago, a school bus full of children was hit by a train in a terrible accident.

Apparently the bus had stalled on the tracks. I'm not sure how this started but, if you go to this crossing and put your car in neutral the car will move over the cross on its own. Or so it would seem.

Many people have done this, and all with the same result. They have put baby powder on the trunk of the car, and you can see the handprints of children pushing the car to safety, so as to save them from the fate they suffered.

It pains me though, because people do this for amusement, especially on Halloween. Their souls will never be given the respect and rest they deserve, because the living don't care about the children of the railroad. ■

It Wasn't Her
Lake Jackson, Texas

It was quite a few years ago, maybe when I was eleven or twelve, when I had my encounter. It didn't seem so troubling then, but now I'm always wracking my brain for some sort of explanation.

I was sleeping over at a friend's house, like I usually did every weekend. There was the occasional bump in the night and unexplained noise, but I always dismissed it. I was young, and what didn't scare me then frightens me now.

It was around five or six in the morning, just at the peek of daylight, when I woke up to see my friend wasn't beside me anymore. Still somewhat asleep, I got up to see where she had gone. In my friend's house, they had sort of a 'junk' nook, where everyone just kept their things in. It was still dark in the house, but in that room nestled in the nook I found my friend. I crouched down next to her and asked what she was doing. Slowly, her head turned and she looked at me. Finally, she replied, "nothing". I shrugged it off and left her, I was cold and wanted to get back to bed.

I went back to her room to see that she was still in bed, sound asleep. Still half asleep, I thought nothing of it and crawled back into bed and fell asleep. There were no other kids in the house, and there was no way she could have sneaked by me to get back to her room. I always thought nothing of it when I was younger. But as I grew up, that memory has always stuck with me, and always made me wonder, just who exactly was I talking to?

Angels Everywhere
Denton, Texas

I have had a lot of very strange things happen that have saved my life at least 30 or more times in the 50 years I have lived.

The only explanation is the feeling I get just after each time it happens. I get this very emotional feeling and many times a picture in my mind of the relative who just snatched me out of the jaws of death. It is always a relative who is already dead.

The most memorable one:

I was 19, and stepping off a curb to cross a street late at night. I was all alone, or so I thought. Suddenly someone grabbed the back of my coat and dragged me backwards onto the curb - just having seconds to save me from a speeding car that was coming down the street at about 70 miles an hour. They were drunk and swerving badly.

As I stood on the curb, in shock, I turned around to see who had grabbed and pulled me back. No one was there! At first I felt a chill, but then I felt this strange warmth and saw an image of my grandfather deep inside of me. It was very strange but not scary. Since then, someone has yanked the steering wheel of my car, saved me from a carjacking, and dozens more incidents. These have assured me each time that I am supposed to stick around awhile longer.

In The Dark
San Antonio, Texas

This story doesn't have a time because it still goes on. But it all began when I was 14 and my cousin moved in for her senior year while her mom moved to another town for a new job.

My cousin moved into the room across from mine, and every weekend my aunt would come down so they could spend time together until she went to college. When she graduated and moved out, that's when I decided to move into her room, because it was bigger.

Well my parents decided to buy me new stuff, so while we were moving things I stayed in the room my aunt used for the year. And weird things happened. First I'd get these sick disturbing images of my dog being ripped to shreds and me being forced to watch it, or my worst fears coming to life.

Then it just stopped and my vision would go. My voice would go, and then I was paralyzed. I couldn't move, I couldn't think, but fear took over my body. And then I could see again.

Black figures were floating above me, laughing and taunting me as if they'd won. I was raised in a religious home and I tried to remember verses, but they were all jumbled up and I couldn't say anything.

I tried screaming for my mom with nothing coming out. So I decided to just scream in my head things I learned at church or from my parents, then it would be over. And I wouldn't be able to go to sleep for the rest of the night.

It happens still to this day, and I'm grown now. I only get these experiences in my aunt's room and my new room. Nowhere else in the house do I feel this uneasy feeling or fear of what's lurking in the dark. Whatever it or they are, they aren't going away, no matter what my parents or I do. I sleep with a Bible every night, hoping it will help, but mostly I've become an insomniac.

The Non-smoker
Houston, Texas

I was only fifteen years old and I lived with my parents.

I should mention that, at only fifteen, I had a very bad smoking problem. Yes, I did consider myself to be addicted. I am very ashamed, I will admit. My parents did not know that I smoked. I usually did it when they were in bed and I was in my bedroom.

On our first night in this house, I was kind of nervous, to say the least. I mean, new house and all... you can't help but feel a little weird. So, I decided at about 1:00 in the morning to have a cigarette... I sneaked one from my mom's pack, and took it into my bedroom. I lit it up and started to relax, when all of the sudden my door started to open! Thinking it was my parents, I quickly put the cigarette out and ran to the door. But, when I opened it up the rest of the way, no one was outside.

I figured, "Great, now I have a broken door."

I shook it off and was kind of scared to go out and get another cigarette, so I didn't smoke that night.

The next night came around, and I did my usual sneak and smoke. It happened again. Now, this time I thought it was weird because I saw the doorknob turn. Thinking it was my parents, I again put it out quickly and ran to the door. And again, no one.

Shaken up this time, I wasn't about to go back out and sneak another one. So, once again, for the second night in a row, I went cigarette-less! Now, this same thing happened every night that I did the sneak and smoke for almost two months. And, for a whole two months I didn't get to have one cigarette and I finally dropped the habit.

I later got some information about that house. The lady that lived here before us was about fifty-four years of age when she died. And, here is the freaky part: She died of lung cancer from smoking.

Here is my one question. Could the dead lady have helped me drop my smoking habit by opening my door just a little to make me think that it was my parents, that way I would quit? I like to think so. ■

A Face in the Mirror
Houston, Texas

When I was young I would visit my grandmother's house a lot. Once when my brother and I were spending the night, something happened that I will never forget.

I was about twelve years old and my brother was ten. I woke up Sunday morning around 7:30 and was just laying in bed daydreaming. My brother was still asleep in another bed next to mine. I could see inside the bathroom from where I was laying, and I was kind of looking at the ceiling when something caught my eye. I looked at the bathroom mirror and saw nothing. I told myself that my mind was playing tricks on me.

My gaze drifted for a minute, and when I looked at the mirror again my heart missed a beat. There was a new reflection in the mirror now, but the strange thing was that there was no one to make the reflection. I saw some brown curly hair on the side of the mirror. I shut my eyes for a couple of minutes and told myself that when I open them it will be gone. I opened my eyes and there was someone looking at me in the mirror. If you ask me details I have none to give you because I jumped out of bed so fast and screamed so loud the neighbors came to see what was wrong.

I only know that the face was a young girl, with brown, short, curly hair in sort of an old fashioned cut. I never slept in that room again. ■

Ghost in the Oven
Corpus Christi, Texas

Our family, all ten of us, went to Corpus Christi, Texas for a weekend and rented a room in a new-looking hotel.

We hadn't planned to get a room since it's more expensive to rent on the spur if the moment. But, we didn't want to do eight total hours driving to go home and come back. We started checking rates along the route. Prices were pretty much equal. We chose this fabulous suite that had room enough for all of us.

It had a separate bedroom with a king bed for me and hubby, a queen bed in main room for daughter and her hubby, and for kids. It had a kitchenette complete with a mini dishwasher, fridge, and microwave, even a full sized stove. Both rooms had their own television.

This suite was so nice, so I decided to take pictures. I'll include one so you can judge for yourself or tell me what you see. It was just weird.

Later on that night, we ordered pizzas and then my ten-year-old granddaughter and I went out to the pool and sat in the hot tub. It was heavenly and relaxing to stare up at the beautiful night sky. A million stars overhead, even with the ambient lighting you could still see the stars. A cool sea breeze wafting over us made it perfect.

We got up bright and early the next morning, ate a delicious continental breakfast with so much food that it made the cost of the room worth it. We then checked out and went back to the beach for a second day of sun and fun.

During that previous night, however things weren't so fun. Strange noises kept waking me up.

At first I thought it was the grandkids, but they were all sleeping, as was my daughter. I kept hearing strange popping sounds all night. Finally I gave up trying to sleep and decided to watch television, but it kept changing channels. I figured maybe someone in the room above us was changing their channels and their remote was messing with our television. I finally gave up, switched it off and lay back down on the luxurious cotton sheets and fluffy comforter.

One thing I can say for sure is that hotel chain, they had the best quality bedding of any hotel I've ever been in. Just wish the other stuff wouldn't have happened,

When we got home I downloaded all the pictures and was surprised to see what looked like a face in the oven door.

You just never know who or what is sharing the room with you, do you? ■

House of Horrors
Denton, Texas

My uncle lived in a house in Denton some 26 years ago with his good friend. The house was at the corner of Ponder and Scripture streets. Odd? When they began to fix the house up, things started happening. One day they heard all sorts of banging and crashing in the shed out back. When they got out there, nothing was awry, except that all the paint cans were tossed onto the floor while not even dust was disturbed.

Faucets would turn on full blast, lights would switch on and off where you could see the switch flipping up and down, radios and TVs would come on.

One day they came home and the dog was inside shaking uncontrollably. The dog hated to be in the house, but refused to go out back. Just then every window flew open, mind you they had all been stuck shut from paint and nails. A huge, loud wind howled through the house. When it settled down, they went out back and found a perfect rectangle sized grave for the dog. But the missing dirt was nowhere to be found.

Years later when he married and my aunt moved in, the terrifying things continued. They would hear a loud thud and find the keys on the other side of the room from the hook they were hanging on. One day they heard commotion outside and peeked out the window. Some kids were pointing, scared and talking and then took off.

When they went outside, a blood-like substance was dripping from all of the eaves.

The final straw happened one night when my uncle was watching TV in the dark living room. He heard footsteps approach him and then something blew the foulest breath in his face. Not knowing what else to do, he rebuked the spirit in Jesus' name and demanded it to leave. My cousin, who I am close to, was a baby at the time, and my aunt and uncle thought the house was too unsafe, so they moved.

My cousin and I are in our mid to late twenties now and her dad still hates to talk about that house. These were the only stories he would share with us. I often wonder who else has lived there since and what they may have experienced.

Mommy
Keller, Texas

My mom killed herself a year ago with a gun. I was sad and I wanted to talk to her again until one night. My mom killed herself in the house we lived in, and one night I was laying in my bed when the light of my digital clock went off. I sat up. Then, my bedroom light turned on for a second and turned off. I heard breathing beside me. I was too scared to move.

The lights turned back on again and at the same time I heard a gun go off. I turned my head to the side. My mom was lying next to me with a bullet hole in her head, and a gun in her hand.

I screamed, and then she said, "What's wrong?"

The lights turned back off again and then turned on. When they did, I was alone in my room as if nothing ever happened.

Baptize me, PLEASE
Austin, Texas

I use to not believe in ghosts, until I stayed at my grandma's house to work on my memory book. In the memory book, I included a picture of my family tree. When we came to my great grandma Frieda, who died of tuberculosis in 1941, my grandma told me a story of an encounter my Aunt Diane had with her.

My Aunt Diane kept seeing a woman in the middle of the night, standing at the foot of her bed, looking right at her. The woman's mouth was moving, but she wasn't making any sound. This went on several times a month for years. Aunt Diane was terrified, but there was nothing to be done except to pull up the covers and shake in fear. She saw doctors, she even saw a psychiatrist, but nothing helped. Nothing stopped the visits.

Then one day Aunt Diane was going through an old family album. She suddenly nearly fainted, and had to lie back on the couch for several minutes. She had recognized the woman from her midnight visits. It was Great Grandma.

When my great-grandma died in 1941, she was unbaptized. In my religion we can go and get baptized for the dead. So she went to the temple and was baptized for her, and never saw her grandma again.

When Great Grandma was mouthing silent words, standing in that dark bedroom over a period of years, she wanted to be baptized. I wonder why? What was there out there, after death, that caused her to spend years seeking baptism? ∎

Little Girl in the Hallway
Houston, Texas

It started right after we bought our home seven years ago. One night, while completely alone in the house, I was in bed watching television. I felt someone watching me, and when I turned my head to the right there stood a little girl of about twelve. She just stood there looking at me. When I got up, she disappeared.

Weeks later, a friend was over at my house around 10:30 at night. My husband was asleep in the bedroom. My friend and I were sitting in the living room, when all of a sudden she looked over and said, "hi". I explained that my husband was asleep, and my friend said she thought she saw someone looking through the living room door. A few minutes later she called out again, because she again thought she saw my husband.

We always see people wandering through my hallway, and they only go one direction. It is very scary. ∎

Voice in My Room
Houston, Texas

One morning at about 8:30, when I was 12 years old, I was lying on the top bunk in my bedroom. My sister had left the bottom bunk and was out in the living room with the rest of my family.

I heard a rustling sound from the floor, and thought it was one of my cats playing with something down there.

I said, "Is that you, kitty?" Obviously I wasn't expecting an answer back.

But immediately in reply, I heard the voice of an old woman say, "No, it's me, Honey." I freaked and looked down to see that nobody was in my room.

I have heard voices in the house since then, but that was the most obvious and frightening. ■

The Rocking Chair
Houston, Texas

I am in possession of the only remaining piece of furniture that was owned by my deceased grandfather. He was a police officer in Houston and retired in 1972. He died in 1981 in his home in a very small town outside of Houston.

The circumstances of his death are not pleasant to remember, so I will not indulge the graphic details. I did however hear his last phone call to my mother and I also heard him die. It is something that will always be in my memory.

After he died, my grandmother refused to ever set foot back in the house and everyone pretty much divided the house. I was only eleven at the time, so a lot of the details are sketchy in my memory.

My father got a couple of items out of the house, including a set of rocking chairs that belonged to my grandparents. The chair belonging to my grandmother broke about eight or so years later, however, the one belonging to my grandfather was still operational, so my father chose to keep it, but placed it in the garage because my mom redid the den.

A few years after that, it was time for me to move out on my own, and so I asked my father if I could use the chair at my house. He agreed and told me to take care of it. This was one of my prized possessions. No one was allowed to sit in the chair other than myself. I still remember my grandfather rocking me in that chair.

A few more years passed, and I got married and had a child. My marriage was not one that I would call very happy. In fact, it was bad. My now ex-husband and I fought often. He worked nights and would have to leave by about 10:15 pm to go to work. Well, at 10pm COPS (the TV show) came on and it's something that I watched regularly. Most of the time I would watch from my grandfather's chair... except for the first night he came to visit me.

I had an argument with my now-ex, as usual, around the time that the show started, but soon after that he left to go to work. I was stretched out on the couch this night because of the draft in the room from the fireplace flue being open. I had covered up with a blanket and was watching the show.

Out of the corner of my eye I saw the chair move. I figured it had been a breeze from the fireplace. I watched the chair moving slightly for the entire length of the show. As soon as it was over, the chair stopped rocking.

The next night there was no argument, but as soon as my ex left, the chair began to rock slightly again. This time I knew that it wasn't from the fireplace because the flue had been closed. Again after the show was over it stopped. This went on for about a week or so and I didn't tell anyone about it. I thought that people would think I had gone crazy.

About three days later, my husband had the night off and was in the den watching "Cops" with me. An argument ensued and not only did the chair rock, but it rocked violently, almost lifting the legs off the floor. My husband was facing it at the time and I had my back to it. I was standing about four feet away.

All of the color left my husband's face and he stopped yelling briefly. I asked him what the problem was. He told me to turn around. When I did, I saw why he looked so stunned. It shocked me and I ran to the other side of the room.

I yelled across the room, "Grandpa stop it!"

Immediately the chair stood still. I knew then for sure why the chair was rocking, and who was rocking it. I had always had my suspicions, but was never sure. This answered my question. My ex asked me how long this had been going on and I told him that it started after the last fight we had. It happened every night after that, but it had never rocked like that before. I also informed him that he must have really pissed my grandpa off!

The chair continued rocking off and on for a long time, but only during police-type shows. Remember, he was a police officer. It never bothered me after that, but I chose to make a phone call to my grandmother in California. She had moved there six months after his death. I told her about what had been going on. She told me a few things that kinda took me by surprise.

First, she told me that my grandfather loved me very much. Much more than some of the other grandchildren and that he had never rocked any of the other kids. Just me. I was the oldest granddaughter, and I was also adopted by my parents at birth. This I knew, but I had never known how excited he had been about me, and how he was so scared that my birth mother would come back and try to get me. He had even devised a plan to hide me from her in that case. I was completely unaware of any of this.

She also told me that he had come to her in her dreams almost nightly since this had all started. She said that he told her to call my father and have him check on me. She never did call my father. She just thought of it as a dream and had no idea of what had been going on. My ex made sure that none of the arguments that we had after that ever occurred around the chair or during police shows.

It was about a month later when I came into the den to watch TV and something happened that chilled me to the bone. That day, not unlike others, I had an argument with my ex. He had left early that night. I was glad that he went. I came into the room and started talking to the chair. I told my grandfather that I wished he was here, to help me be stronger and get my ex out of my life. I left the room during a commercial and had gotten the afghan my grandmother had made me to use as a throw over the chair. I had used it there before and actually quite often. I threw the afghan over the top of the chair, only to realize there was the form of a person underneath for a brief moment. Then it went flat.

From that day on I always kept something in the chair when it wasn't being used. A stuffed animal or folded clothes or whatever. I also made a phone call to talk to my grandmother and asked her to please talk to him about his visits and to please make them not so frequent. She said that she would, and apparently it worked. He would only come occasionally from then on. Usually only when I felt down or was upset or something.

I divorced my husband shortly after that and started a new life. I never told my new husband about the chair. He was at home alone one evening and decided to straighten up the bedroom (where I had put the chair). He had taken all of the items out of the chair and got into bed and started watching Law and Order. Guess who came to visit?! That's right. He came back to visit.

I then received a phone call to come home immediately. I came home to the story and a look of astonishment on my new husbands face. I assured him that it was all right, but to always leave an item in the chair.

We moved about six months ago, and there was no room for the chair in the new house. It now resides in my storage shed. I refuse to throw it away. I might want to visit with my grandfather again some day. By the way this is the only existing piece of furniture left from my grandfather. ■

Boy that Died in a Fire
Corpus Christi, Texas

My family of six moved into a beautiful three-bedroom house. We were all excited about the new home. At that time my parents were having financial problems, so when we moved into this big three bedroom house we were all happy... not knowing what was to come out of that nice house.

Behind our house was a small guesthouse that was burned down.

Three days after settling in the home it started. After midnight every night the door to the bathroom would open up and you could hear the toilet flushing.

My sisters and I shared a room right beside the bathroom. We would get scared and cover our face with the blankets until we fell asleep.

A week after we were living there, my seven-year-old brother would sit in the living room floor and talk to someone that wasn't there. My mother would ask him who he was talking to, and he would say, "My friend."

We really didn't pay any mind to that. We thought he was just being a kid with an imaginary friend... until we all saw him throwing a ball across the room and the ball wouldn't hit the floor. The ball was being thrown back at him.

We all got so scared that my mother arranged for a preacher to come and bless the house, but it would be a week until he could come. So, my mother brought a lady over that was supposed to be psychic. She walked through the house and stopped in the middle of the hallway and started talking to the spirit, asking him why was he there and what did he want.

She told my mother that he had died in the guesthouse behind our house, and he just wanted to play with my baby brother.

We were all so scared; we all slept in my mother's room. The preacher came over and blessed the house, but it didn't work because my brother was still playing with him. You could even see that someone was jumping on the sofa but no was there.

We ended up moving out a month later. We were all too scared to stay there and scared that something would happen to my brother.

I wonder of that boy is still there. We never went back to that house.

Apartment 1204
Houston, Texas

This particular story happens to be one of many encounters that I experienced. I come from a family with 3 sisters that are all attuned to these, what should we call them? Happenings?

From 2002 through May of 2004 my husband and I were living in an apartment on the north side of Houston. One evening while in the kitchen together cleaning up after dinner, our cat George came wandering in to eat his own dinner. While standing there I became very uneasy and had a feeling someone was watching me. I looked up to see the same unease apparent on my husband's face. George too felt something and puffed up his hair and his eyes went wide with fright. All three of us -- the two wary humans, and one scaredy cat -- looked toward the entrance of the kitchen and felt such a powerful need to flee! The cat, of course, ran out first but was quickly followed by my husband and myself. What it was we did not know but felt that whatever it was wanted us gone.

Our logical brains of course tried to dismiss this as all a part of our imagination. However, a few months later cleaning up in the kitchen by myself I looked up from my scrubbing to peer in the mirrored backsplash. Seeing a man walking down the hallway from the living room towards me I saw an opportunity to catch my husband as he tried to sneak up on me. You see he likes to startle me... he thinks it's funny. So I wheeled around with my hands out and ready to proclaim - Ha! I got you! I see only the empty hall. What I did see at the end if the hall was my husband sitting in a chair in front in the TV, playing a video game... and wearing headphones!

Our two years living in this apartment, we never slept

with the door open from our bedroom that leads to the hall and to the kitchen.

It always felt like someone was watching us. We also argued and went through toughest times in our marriage while living there. The apartment was so full of negativity.

Our last night in the apartment... we had our moving truck all packed up for the big move to New York so very few items were left. We were squaring away for the evening... so we brushed our teeth and put away our toothbrushes and paste in the medicine cabinet. We were setting up the air mattress in the living room and I walked into the bedroom to grab the pillows. As a fitting goodbye and good riddance our toothbrushes were sitting on our pillows. ■

Something in the House: The Little Girl
Seadrift, Texas

There have been times when you feel like someone's in the house, but you dismiss as, "I'm just scaring myself, no one is here." Sometimes that is not the case.

I grew up in an old two-story Victorian style house. My brother David seemed to have extreme things happen to him there. (See that story, "Something in the House". As well as has the rest of my family.

My story isn't as intense as his, but still unexplainable. I was around 14-15 when this happened to me.

I was sleeping down stairs; the room I was in was the living room that was separated by the hallway with two glass French doors. At night I would shut the big wooden front door, as well as any doors in the hall way and turn on all the lights. I developed this habit when we started hearing strange noises in the house.

I had laid on the couch watching movies in hope that I would eventually fall asleep. My dad was asleep upstairs and had been asleep for several hours. As I started to drift off to sleep I heard what sounded like someone walking around upstairs with dress shoes on. They were just walking back and forth. When I looked at the clock it showed 12 o'clock.

"What is dad doing walking around upstairs with dress shoes on this late?" I wondered. The reason I thought this was because dress shoes make a particular sound on hard wood floors. The sound continued for another minute or two, then just stopped.

I stared into the hallway until my nerves settled a bit. I couldn't sleep after that. I couldn't convince myself it was just my dad. So I searched for a different movie that would bore me to sleep. Thirty minutes later I started to feel more at ease and relaxed enough to close my eyes.

Then the noise started again, but this time on the stairs. The steps were quickened and it sounded like some running up and down the stairs. The problem was is that the end of the stairs is so close to the French doors that led to the room I was sleeping in. I shot my head up expecting my dad to be going into the bathroom. However there was no one!

I sat up and told myself that I had to check to make sure! I was almost too freaked out to check, so I convinced myself dad was in the bathroom. As I knocked on the wooden bathroom door I was hoping to hear "yeah?" from my dad. When I opened the bathroom door it was dark with no one in there. I frantically rechecked all the doors in the hallway, making sure each one was properly shut.

I finally was able to go back to the couch, once I felt that everything was secure. I stayed up for another two hours. I knew that I had to find a way to go to sleep, so I laid down, covered myself with the covers and pushed my face into the crease of the couch. I slowly started to close my eyes when what sounded like a ton of books was slammed beside my head!

I shot my head up expected someone or something to be inches away from my head. No one was there, no books, nothing was out of place. My heart raced, someone doesn't want me to sleep. So I didn't. I stayed up until the light outside gradually got brighter. I didn't want to find out what would happen next if I chose to ignore the thing creating all the sounds.

I told my mom the next day what happened and she said it was probably "that little girl". Apparently she always wanted to play with my brother and I when we were little kids. I later found out that she died in our house and was kept in the closet underneath the stairs. My mom has said that she has seen her. She wore a dirty white dress and looked like she had been neglected. I guess all she wanted was someone to pay attention to her.

Cemetery Incident
Houston, Texas

I lived in a small town a little south of Houston. The city was built in the area of an old Indian burial ground, so a lot of places were known to be haunted.

When I was in high school, my friends and I bought a glow in the dark Ouija board and decided to play with it one night.

I knew of an old cemetery that not a lot of people knew about. It was on a hill by a creek and to get there you had to take back roads. We thought this would be a good place to play. One of my friends had the sixth sense and was on the Montel show for it, so she came along.

We played on top of the hood of my car right along the edge of the cemetery. We picked up a spirit of a four-year-old boy but he only gave us his initials. He said that he was buried alive and that's how he died.

Just then the wind picked up and we heard crackling and whistling as if someone was behind us in the forest. The street we were on was dividing the cemetery from the forest. We asked the boy if he was making the noise and he said yes. We then asked if he was going to hurt us and he said yes. At this point we stopped playing and threw everything in the car and got out of there.

We were all scared. On the way back home we were driving, still scared, when all of a sudden we heard a big crash from inside the car. I asked, "What the heck was that?"

and my friend said the pointer from the game just flew across the car and hit the door! If you heard the crash you would know that that piece had to have had a lot of force behind it.

So we stopped and decided to talk to the boy so he would leave us alone. We asked it what he wanted us to do and he started to spell D-I and then we all took our hands off cause we knew he was spelling die. We then prayed to lift his spirit up and dismissed the spirit then we threw the game in the dumpster.

Never doing that again. ■

Oh, That's Just My Dead Sister
Wichita Falls, Texas

My Nana used to have a sister but she died from pneumonia when she was only 3 years old. My family (especially my Nana) believes she comes out and warns us when something bad is about to happen. I didn't believe this was true until it actually happened to me.

One night my Nana, my mom, my aunt Sandy, and my aunt Suzan were playing poker in our dining room. I was in the living room just across from the dining room watching television, and I see a girl who looked kind of like my youngest sister come in the room. She was wearing a white nightgown, but looked too young to be Rae (my littlest sister) so I figured it was one of her friends.

I asked her what was wrong and she walked out of the room into the den, which was at the back of the house. I noticed our sliding glass door was opened so I went outside expecting to find my dog, but he wasn't there. I wandered around the backyard for a bit until I noticed our gate was open. Quickly I ran into the house to find my dog. He wasn't there. I ran back outside to find the girl standing right next to my dog (who had run out the gate). I thanked the girl and picked up the dog, but when I turned around to ask her who she was, no one was there.

Puzzled, I went back inside and told my Nana what had happened; she asked me if she was young and blonde. I responded yes. She smiled and said, "That's my dead sister! She died when I was seven."

I have always been interested in the paranormal, and believe that I am psychic, but I never thought your own family could warn you if anything bad happened. Believe me or not I truly believe my Nana's dead sister is my family's guardian angel. ∎

Black Magic
College Station, Texas

My grandma never liked my mother, not even after she married my father. There was always a weird feeling that my grandma gave off around my mother.

I was born a year after my parents got married and was a quiet well behaved child- well at least until my dad came back from a trip from India (my grandma lives there). He came back with a black kar (rope-like thing that could be both good and bad). Within a day I was throwing tantrums and screaming. Soon enough I lost it somewhere and I was back to normal.

Within a year my grandma sent one again (this time for everyone) and there was a repeat of the family destruction. The next few times they were sent, none of us wore them and every thing went back to normal.

The next year, my dad invited my grandparents to stay with our family for a year. They accepted. Two months after their arrival, my mom and I were in a car crash. It was bad and we were lucky that we survived. My grandma came to visit us in the hospital with flowers. I remember that exact day. She smiled and told me I was going to be okay. Then she turned and grinned at my mom and walked up to her, put her hand on my mom's head and started to whisper. It didn't sound like a prayer. It was odd and in a different tone.

There were no more car accidents after that, but our family relationship went downhill. My dad would blame my mom for the accident. My mom would blame my grandparents. My dad knew, but was in denial. My parents fought so much that it sometimes got violent. I prayed for them.

The next target was our new home. This was our first house. It was small but perfect for our family. These were the good days for our family since we bonded. Then our dogs started running out into the backyard, barking. It was as if they were chasing something out of the house. One dog would not enter the bedroom in fear. The other one would bark and get aggressive.

We kept dolls on the top of the fireplace. Their heads would always turn. This may have been because of the vibrations or any other natural cause, but it still freaked us out.

The final step was when one day I brought in the newspaper to give to my dad. He took it and opened it. On it there was a huge splash of red. It was not ink. In Indian black magic, lemons, sindoor (red stuff), and blood are all used. This freaked my mom out.

She did a puja (kind of like how the priest bless the house) -a religious prayer to get rid of spirits. It seemed to work since we even got a candle footprint in our driveway. It was stepping out of the house. It wasn't normal-sized. It was small. Again, everything was normal.

My grandma kept sending religious items to us, but we always threw them away. This was done mostly without my dad's knowledge.

Everything was normal until a few months ago. I kept on seeing things. Not ghosts or dead people, but movements in the corner of my eyes. I get weird scary feelings at random times. At times I can't wake up from sleep. They are not nightmares, but I feel frozen.

I do not know what I will do. I talked to my mom. She will get professional help for us (me) as soon as she figures out who to go to.

Child In The Hallway Bathroom
Houston, Texas

When I was a child, my father had a house by a lake, which we would go visit every summer. I loved it, but there was something that bothered me about it. It had a dark hallway that led to the bathroom. As a little girl, every time I would pass by there to go use it I would feel like something was watching me, and not something good.

One day as I was walking down I felt a blast of hot air that smelled of death and sorrow. I can't explain how I know but I just know. Then I continued walking, but afraid out of my wits. Just as I was about to put my hand on the doorknob of the bathroom door, I felt a hand push me back and at that moment I heard something that chilled me. It was the scream of a child but unworldly. I had enough. That moment I turned and ran for my life. I caught a glimpse of what was in the bathroom and to this day it still scares me. It was a young girl about 6 or 7. She had scars all over her body. She was naked and bleeding but her eyes were what almost stopped me. They were black and full of sadness and despair, but at the same time with a cold calculating look that seemed too smart for a little girl.

I'll probably never know what happened there but I do know this that thing, whatever it was, was real and evil. I could feel it.

2:10 AM
Lake Jackson, Texas

I have been reading these ghost stories a lot lately and a lot of them I can blatantly tell they are demons attacking people. Being a strong Christian and very firm in my faith I have been reading the stories and thinking I could deal with such a situation.

Well for about three weeks I have been waking up at 2:10 AM exactly. Not exactly scary, but just kinda weird and annoying. Well last night I went to bed knowing well I was most likely going to wake up at 2:10 and was ready just to suck it up and go back to bed.

Last night was different. I woke up with my TV blaring sound. I thought rationally. I must have laid on the remote, turning the volume up all the way. I lay listening to the loud TV while an infomercial was yelling at me about fitness. Then suddenly the woman's voice on the infomercial began gargling. I thought it was just the speakers messing up. Then the voice began getting lower and lower, until I could only describe it as demonic speaking, something I didn't understand. Freaked at this I panicked and jumped out of the bed. The TV was on with the infomercial, but the demonic voice was coming from something else.

I gathered myself. I began praying and yelling at the demon, "In Jesus' name you have no power over me! And in Jesus' name you are banished from this house!" and as soon as I said this everything had stopped. My TV was muted. Everything was quiet.

The next morning I asked my mom why she didn't check on me and she said she heard nothing. I know I was fully awake because I went and got some orange juice. Now I know I can take on anything that may attack me in the night. ■

Madonna
Spring, Texas

I've had many experiences in my lifetime that can only be described as strange to say the least. Most of them happened when I was younger.

My grandmother raised me, and I think many of my experiences were due to the weird items she collected in her travels as a colonel's wife.

Growing up with these things seemed normal at the time, but in hindsight there was nothing normal about them.

There was a huge wrought-iron clock with roman numerals running backwards... at the bottom of this clock was an ugly gargoyle with outstretched wings and fangs.

There was a shelf with another horrid creature posed underneath the flat part of the shelf with its legs drawn up and wings outstretched, a small statue of a woman holding (what I thought) were blue eggs... no they are her eyes... you get the picture. *Strange* stuff.

This story revolves around one of the items that most would consider mild compared to the rest. It was a print of the Madonna and child inside an ornate gold frame and matted (I guess) with an oval mat.

My grandmother hung this print in my bedroom and from the day it was hung there I experienced scary stuff! I heard echoing voices that I couldn't make out, but they sounded like a group of people arguing in an empty metal barrel. And I thought Mary and the Christ child were watching me, so I would put my pajamas on out of their sight.

I also became very sick several times but my grandmother was of a faith that did not believe in going to doctors. Instead, if someone is very sick, a church practitioner will visit and pray... I awoke to the 93rd Psalm more times than I care to remember.

Eventually I convinced my grandmother to remove the print from my room and she hung it in hers.

I found this out much later: my step grandfather and my grandmother on separate occasions awoke to see a demonic face within the oval mat! My step grandfather insisted it be removed from their room!

It now hangs in the home of my step mom (my dad passed away several years ago). No one has experienced anything abnormal since its been hung there.

Joe Kwon's True Ghost Stories

The Haunted Doll
Livingston, Texas

Hi! I'm Shannon. I'm 30 years old, and I want to tell you a story. When I was about the age of 9, my Aunt passed away. She left behind her six-year-old daughter, my cousin Sarah, for my grandparents to raise.

My grandparents lived (well my grandma still does) in a two-story house. The second story, many years ago, used to be a garage apartment. My grandparents bought it and made it into a two-story house. Ok that's a little background info to help you follow me better.

So, about a year after my Aunt's death, me, cousin Sarah, my mom, my grandma and grandpa, and my great grandma decided to leave early one summer morning and go to Galveston, Texas, to spend the day at the beach.

We were gone all day, not returning home until after dark. Now, my Aunt who passed on had a doll that my grandma had given her when she was a child. This doll, if you put it up to baby pictures of my aunt, looks freakishly like her. And my grandma used to make their clothes and would dress my aunt and the doll alike. Sarah was given this doll after her mother died and by this point the doll was like 25 years old or so and its head wouldn't even stay up. It just flopped over.

Ok, so back to my story. The doll was upstairs in Sarah's room, and my grandma had set it up in a little metal kids' chair and placed it in front of the window at the corner of the bunk beds.

So, no one had been home all day, and Sarah and I were the first to run upstairs to shower off because we had sand all over us. We jumped in the shower together, both being kids and girls, and washed off. We got out of the shower, grabbed towels to wrap around ourselves, and headed into Sarah's room to dry off and get dressed. We were chatting away about our day at the beach when, in the middle of throwing on pajamas, we both froze!

We looked at each other, chills running through both of us, and then turned to look back at the doll.

For a moment we couldn't move. There was her mother's creepy doll sitting on the top bunk next to the window, with its feet dangling off the side.

No one had been in that house all day and us two were the first to go upstairs after returning that evening. We both turned and ran down the stairs! No one believed us then, and to this day they still don't.

They always just laugh. But that doll has creeped me out for years. ∎

Man in the Hall
Peaster, Texas

My husband has told this story several times. He is the oldest of four boys. While living with his parents as a child, about 9 or 10 years old, he awoke suddenly one night. He sat straight up in bed. He called to all three brothers (they all slept in the same room in bunk beds), but no one answered. As he lay back down, a man in his thirties, wearing a plaid shirt and puffed vest, walked toward him smiling. What is strange is that he could see him because the closet light was on.

Now, if you know my father in law, he always says the furniture doesn't need light. So the boys always turned off all of the lights. He says the man had a huge grin on his face. He never spoke, just smiled, walked up to the bed, turned and walked through the window to the outside.

A few nights later, the same thing happened. He woke up suddenly out of a dead sleep, the closet light was on, and he could see this man smiling at him. The only difference was that now he had brown hair rather than blonde. He walked to him, grinning, turned, and walked down the dark hallway.

My (now) husband jumped out of bed and shook the three other boys to no avail. No one would come to. Terrified, he weighed the decision whether or not to cross the dark hallway to his parents' room. No one would wake up. He made himself go back to sleep, only telling his family the next morning.

His parents mentioned that the animals had been acting very strangely in the previous days. A few days later, his dad found something and asked the boys where it came from.

"It's a good luck token from our friend down the road," the boys replied.

Their dad said to them, "This has a satanic symbol on it, and we will not have this in our home, get rid of it! Now I know why things have been weird lately."

Upon hearing this, the boys tried to return the thing, but of course hearing the story, the boy didn't want it back. They tossed it out into some pastureland behind their property. A few weeks later the pasture mysteriously caught fire, leaving behind only charred grass. ∎

iPod
Oglesby, Texas

It was basketball season, and I was taking shot charts and listening to my iPod. After the game ended I went home.
As I was laying in bed trying to go to sleep, I remembered that I left my iPod in the bleachers at school. But to make absolutely sure, I tore the whole house apart looking for it.

I never found it, but I had a feeling that everything was going to be okay, so I feel asleep.

When I woke up in the morning and got ready, there was just something telling me that everything was okay. I believed the feeling, and went to school.

The first place I went to was the office and asked if anyone had found an iPod. She said no. So I went to the janitors. Same answer.

So when it was time for first period, I was crying and freaking out. My iPod had information on it that could be used in identity theft.

By this point it was all over school. By the end of the day, when the last bell rang, I went and looked in my mom's car, under the seats and everything. Nothing. Absolutely nothing.

I lost all hope and started setting money aside so I could buy a new one. So just to look one more time, I looked in my living room in every nook and cranny, and nothing.

So I turned on the TV and me and my mom where watching some show, when she said she was going to take a shower and went up stairs. Suddenly feeling really tired, I laid my head down for maybe 5 seconds when something just told me to look up. And there was my iPod laying neatly at the end of the atimund. And I knew I didn't overlook it, because I had turned it over a couple of minutes ago. And I hadn't moved anything or got up since I had flipped it over.

I just knew it had been stolen and that some force beyond this world had brought it back to me. My friends believed me but my teachers thought I was crazy and just made up this whole thing to get attention.

There have been several incidents since then of me losing something and then I'll look again where I just looked, and there it will be.

Blood On The Wall
Dayton, Texas

Mom and I were painting our hallway about six months back. Since our house has had previous stories with it and several experiences we have actually had, I told mom jokingly that since we are doing remodeling we may stir up the spirits. She laughed and said maybe. For awhile we haven't had much happen in our house, I guessed the spirits had gone away.

To get to the story. We were painting over old brown wood paneling. As we were painting there was this blood red color that started seeping through . It was the weirdest thing, and it was in two different spots.

Every time we would paint over it, it would keep bleeding through. It was so strange! It finally went away after we grabbed a crucifix.

Bloody Mary
Houston, Texas

A couple years ago at a day camp, me and my friends were talking about that Bloody Mary game. If anyone doesn't know what that is, its a game that a lot of kids play to try and summon ghosts. You hold hands and chant "Bloody Mary" in front of a mirror in the dark.

Anyway we were talking about it some of us were like, "let's go do it!"

And so we went into the bathroom, which is a really large bathroom, and we turned the lights off. These are by the door and the sink. Then we stood by the back wall. We were about like 20 to 25 feet away from the door, and there were three of us.

I stood in the middle and we all held hands and repeated "Bloody Mary" and all that.

The first time nothing happened to me, but my friend felt a hand on her shoulder and my other friend said it felt like a rat was in her shirt.

Nothing happened to me, so I was like, "This is stupid, and you are just imagining it."

So, we did it again and this time we heard a huge bang, and we screamed and ran over and turned lights on. The huge trash can that was 25 feet away by the sink had fallen over.

We still wanted to do it again, so we did it again. We were standing there and 25 feet away the sink turned on full blast. It was spraying cold water, and it was the kind you have to twist and pull up to turn on. It was twisted and pulled up and of course it hadn't been when we came in.

Then when my friend turned the light on, and the second

she turned it on the water stopped.

Some games you don't want to play.... It might be for keeps. ■

Demon Friend
Austin, Texas

When I was doing laundry I went to my daughter, Sauris's room to gather her dirty clothes. I could hear her faint whispers and giggling. She was my only child, we had no pets, so I assumed she was talking to her doll.

I walked in and proceeded to get her clothes. She turned to look at me, no doll in sight.

"Sauris, who was that?"

She turned away, then stood slowly. Her eyes grew wide and she let out a high, shrill scream that made my heart skip a beat.

Sauris fell to the ground once more, and continued to talk to her "friend." I hurried to my room where my husband was working on the computer.

I immediately shouted, "I need you to ask Sauris about that friend of hers!" I was still worried. Why had she done such a thing? She was always a quiet and calm child. He nodded and went to her room. I waited outside, listening to their every word.

It turned out she had a friend that we couldn't see named Andrew. He made her laugh and played with her. Andrew told her he was going to make her do something and he would have complete control over her. Like, possessing her. I was angry and worried at the same time.

That same night I hurried to put her to bed and she refused to listen to me. She glared in my direction, making a growling noise. "Sauris stop!" I demanded. "Get away!" she screamed and ran to hide in her closet. I could hear heavy breathing coming from the closet.

I then decided I was going to talk to Father Jansen the next morning.

We met at the church in his office, both of us quiet. "Based on what you told me over the phone it sounds like Sauris has a not so nice friend. If she screamed like that and did those things he must have possessed her. Did you do something to upset s spirit?"

I then remembered how tearing down the extra room because of the strange noises had something to do with it. "Father, I think I did upset a demon. My husband and I were tearing down an extra room. The room where the strange noises were... Where that teenage boy killed himself." I sighed.

This happened a time ago, and my daughter has not talked to him since. Turns out I was right. It was a demon and she was possessed.

This is my story and all true. ■

Michelle
Andrews, Texas

I was about 14 years old. My friend Nora and I were curious to play the Ouija board. She pulled it out from under her bed. So, we started playing, and a friend that had just passed away supposedly was talking to us. We stayed up all night talking to him.

The next morning we tried to get back on to talk to him, but instead we contacted a girl named Michelle. She seemed really nice and friendly, and constantly insisted that I knew her. She knew deep secrets about me that no one else knew. So, I asked my friend if I could take the Ouija board with me home.

Well, Rule Number 1 is, when you play the Ouija board don't play with it alone. And of course, stupid, curious me broke the #1 rule, and played it alone.

My friend the next morning called me tripping out. She said that she was asleep on her bed and that she felt something watching her. And a hand came through her window and started choking her. Her mom heard her kicking the wall and ran in her room and saw Nora gasping for air, and freaked out.

Nora told me to throw away the board, but I didn't listen. I played with that board hours a day. To me I felt I found a good friend, until later when weird things started happening to me.

One time my cousin was over, and I was talking to my boyfriend on the phone. All I remember is being in a dark place, and when I came to my cousin was shaking me and my boyfriend was calling out to me over the phone. When I asked them what had happened, they told me that I was somebody else. My voice changed and I was crying and ranting that my dress was full of blood, and I was in pain.

So they freaked out and told me to stop playing the Ouija board. Then the next day my other cousin came over. Her dad passed away when she was 3, and she wanted to talk to him. but something kept interfering in their conversation. It kept asking for me.

So I got on and it spelt, "I'm gonna kill you." When I asked who it was, it spelt the word "Swift." So I freaked out. I let my cousin take it home with her and never touched it again.

But it didn't stop there. At night when I go to sleep I can feel something evil watching over me. I can hear her in the bathroom, in my room, and out my window. I would see her in my dreams, there were times where she even got in my dolls.

And one night I finally had a vision. I saw me in the past of El Paso, Texas. It was the year 1876. My hair was blonde, my eyes were blue, and I was wearing an old peasant dress. I was Michelle, and I saw her being murdered by her ex-fiancé and her cousin (Swift).

Ever since then I still see Michelle and still get more clues of her unsolved murder, and I know somehow or another she wants revenge. A lot more has happened, but it's too long to explain everything. It's been 7 years of visions, dreams, and sightings. I just want to know what she wants from me... ∎

My Cozy Haunted Home
Pampa, Texas

The story is tragic indeed. Eerie sights? Yes! Chilling sounds? Absolutely! A frightening experience to several people? Without a doubt.

I have always enjoyed horror movies, blood, gore, and

other things of the sort. I have always wondered what it would feel like to come face-to-face with a supernatural being: Would I have the heebie-jeebies? Would I feel as if my life were at stake? Would I shriek with terror, only to find no one to help me? What, exactly, could it do to me, besides scare me?

All of these wonders were true to some degree. But, the sense that something was wrong; dreadfully wrong, was the most horrific part. Never, even in my wildest nightmares, did I dream of being directly in the midst of a real-life haunting. Never, in my most lucid thoughts, could I imagine the feeling that would overcome me countless times.

June 2009 was a bright time in my brother's life. After surmounting many personal obstacles, he was off to purchase his first home. I was right by his side as we toured the many homes of his interest. I favored one in particular.

I loved the floor plan, and it had a warm, cozy feeling that the others seemed to lack. But, I spoke nothing of my preference. I crossed my fingers, though. I immensely hoped that he would pick this house. It felt....well.....right. It felt right.

The wood trim surrounding the lower one/third of the living area added a warmth unlike any other. The layout reminded us both of the home of our childhood. I was filled with delight when he chose that house. OH, how cunning and deceitful that warmth was.

The move was soon completed, and he was good and settled. I would go by to visit him each morning and to enjoy the house. Strange how a year later I could hardly set foot near the place.

A couple of months passed, and a medical condition that he had struggled with for countless years began to slowly creep up on him, like a ghost in and of itself.

He was the same person, but not so in many ways. He slept more. His moods were erratic. He lost interest for something he had painstakingly developed a zest for....life itself! Yet, the changes were subtle enough that one would have to know him to see them.

In early fall of 09, I was heavily into writing poetry.

A creative zest was flowing, and I would often go to my brother's warm and comfortable home as a getaway. One night, something did not seem right at the house. It wasn't a sight. It wasn't a sound.

It was more than just a sense. It is impossible to fully explain. An "experience" is the only word I can think of to describe "it". As I was writing in the office, the wall to my right (where the doorway was) was heavily drawing my attention. Nothing unusual about the wall, but it kept distracting me.

Fear can manifest itself in many ways, but what I began to feel at this point was a consumption by fear that is as close to hell as I ever care to get. The distraction of the wall was similar to someone looking over your shoulder while you are trying to concentrate (annoying and intrusive). A transitional phase was occurring and resonating within me. My sensitivity to whatever was in the house was concurrent to the continuing and intensifying intrusiveness of the wall. The wall, as seen from my peripheral vision went from noticeable, to annoying, to frightening. The intensity of the "inner" experience was in correlation with the noticeability of the intrusive, "living" wall.

First of all, everything was backwards: Instead of seeing or hearing something THEN becoming terrified as a reaction, the feeling started from within, like something was upsetting my central nervous system. As I sat in the great office chair, poetry in hand, I began to feel fearfully different. My heart began racing. Again, these happenings were not in response to any exterior happenings. They seemed to originate inside.

Soon, I felt mind altered, as if I were in a serious drug-induced state. I was petrified to move, yet I had to. My tolerance for paranoia and fear gradually reached a ceiling in which, one way or another, I had to leave. I didn't know what any of this meant or where it came from.

The not knowing probably accounts for half of the fear. I simply knew that I had to leave. As I gathered my personal items from the home's kitchen, my eyes were fixated on the mid-sized kitchen windows, and the black of night which they revealed. Paranoia raged through me and left me feeling like a cornered beast with nowhere to run. Windows spooked me to the point of dizziness and faint-like feelings.

Once I made it to my car, I had to sit and calm down for about 15 minutes before feeling safe to drive. The paranoia and tension left me crashed out in exhaustion when I arrived at home. It was as if something was thriving on my energy. Something was draining me in order to revive itself. Once I returned to normal mind, it was as if the whole episode was an insignificant distant nightmare. But this was only the beginning of a series of events which eventually made the house uninhabitable.

I endured similar experiences, at least a dozen more times over the course of the next 9 months. Not the wisest move I've ever made, but I "experimented" if you will, to notice any patterns: I was successful at discovering traits that were common to each "mind altered" event.

First, my brother would be gone from the house OR he would be disconnected from it in some way each time that these episodes occurred. For example, if he went to bed, then the effects began. And their intensity always had to be maximal for me to fleet. If I stayed long enough, it always progressed and became intolerable. I went through this at least 3 times before concluding that, whatever was happening to me, was centered around my brother's presence (or absence).

Due to some health conditions which he was dealing with at the time, I decided to not mention my encounters to him.

One day, while sitting on the porch in early spring, he brought up something in conversation which confirmed my every belief that vividly strange activity was taking place, well beyond my personal experience.

He casually mentioned that he had felt a cold spot. Not a rush of wind, like from an air conditioner, but a solid, concentrated cold body. which would approach him from the guest area (near the office wall), and then return, rushing through him once more, on its way back to the guest area.

The most disturbing and eerie event that he disclosed was hearing a dismembered and extremely violent voice call his name from the dark guest hallway one night. It shrieked his name, disguised in my dad's voice. My dad is still alive, by the way. He seemed strangely unbothered by these happenings.

So, at this point, I concluded that the house was indeed occupied by something supernatural.

Since then, several claims have been brought to my attention. We (my family) agreed to remain very "hushed" about the situation as we discussed and accepted the goings on.

The housekeeper, who is amazingly immaculate in her work, was slacking off from her usual standards. Some rooms remained unclean, and she often seemed "in a rush" to get her work done. I called on her to meet with me. I asked, first of all, if she was bothered by something while cleaning the house. She emphatically said yes.

She explained how she had a strong sense of "being watched." She was cleaning the guest bathroom one day, and had an overwhelming sense of a dooming presence. She whirled around to see a dark shadow behind the shower curtain. She immediately fled the house.

In order to continue working there, She brought her daughter to work with her, opened all blinds, doors, and turning on the television. She claimed to have felt the energy still, but it was more at bay.

Next, of all people, a banker who makes occasional visits stopped by the house to see my brother. As she passed the "haunted hallway" near the home's entrance, she jumped back towards the door (about three steps), as if it were a knee-jerk reaction. Her intuitions told her she did not need to be there, so she stated a few pleasantries to my brother and left immediately.

Another account: "Bob," a professional alcohol/drug interventionist, was hired to help a family member. He was staying in the guest room. He had the ghost radar app on his phone (One which I have come to believe is truly legitimate). I explained to him, from personal experience, that something, be it a ghost, spirit, or far worse, was concentrated in that part of the house. I had used such a device, and it annoyed the presence and in turn "tripled" the negative oppression. The entity (or whatever you want to call it), did NOT like devices that exposed it.

Also, I had a bottle of Holy water but was instructed to

not try and rid the presence on my own. I was, furthermore, told that I should wait until I knew exactly what I was dealing with.

Bob continued to use the radar device and, as was the case when I once used it, felt the intensity of the waxing entity.

One morning, I made my usual visit, to astonishingly find that most of the Holy water was gone. I entered the office area to find the place literally "drenched" with the sacred water, crooked lampshades, as well as other displaced items. The computer keyboard was sopping wet as well as the beautifully furnished desk.

Shockingly, I soon discovered Bob: He was slobbering, babbling, and barely able to stand. Unfortunately, he had a major relapse into dangerously intense drug use (while serving as an interventionist) and was in need of immediate medical care. After working with his supervisor, we were able to stabilize the ever-increasing tumultuous situation.

My thoughts: He surpassed his tolerance level to whatever force was present in the house, especially in his room, by "teasing" it with the device. Frightened, he doused the place with nearly a half-gallon of the sacred water. This, as well, could have (and I believe did), been the final act which set the entity off. Thank God he survived the relapse.

I met with the local paranormal society. I always imagined dark suits, or gothic-like attire, when it came to individuals who vastly pursued the paranormal. They were everyday people. My obvious anxiety was calmed by their reassurance that all would be well.

They felt the forces in the house the instant that they entered. They immediately noted the strong vibes coming from the dark guest area. For the sake of accuracy, we didn't discuss specifics prior to their investigation.

They had a demonologist along for the walk-through, and I was relieved to hear him say that, for certain, no demons were present. They noted that the house was not just haunted by one ghost, but by several! They scheduled a second meeting in which "anything goes" as far as the ghosts were concerned: (When they are forced from their hiding and demanded to leave, they WILL reveal themselves. I was told this by the Paranormal group.)

The evening came, September 11, 2010, and the amount and the visual and listening devices were amazing. The videography device was sensitive to the point of picking up the sight of dust. Before the session even began, we could see orbs moving across the room on the video set-up. They seemed to be shooting out of the guest area.

The work began, and a psychic was present. Within minutes of being inside of the house, she ran, pushing through the group of paranormal agents to exit the house. I was outside watching the video and she stormed out, out of breath and extremely frightened.

She verily asked about my brothers whereabouts and insisted on meeting with him. The meeting was not possible, but she put her arm on me and reiterated numerous times that, if the house remained "uncleaned" then he was for certain to die as a result of his condition. His sickness caused weakness and opened him up to the energy-seeking entities in the house.

Obviously, that was extremely disturbing to me. I had no idea what to do for him except sell the house. I just decided to wait and discover the results of the cleaning.

Backing up a day or so, I had to collect some personal items for my brother. I had my nephew with me, and we decided to turn our iPhone ghost radars on. We decided to use his device since I was considered an intruder as a result of my authority over my brother. Strange, it spoke, but only when addressed directly.

We asked if "whatever was there" had a name. The radar immediately responded audibly with "Henry." Next, knowing he was likely a Native American via the paranormal society, we had picked out a phrase of words which interpreted "we come as friends." We stated the phrase, and "Henry" immediately stated "equal."

Obviously, to us, he was stating that he, too, came as a friend. He made a few more statements, and I sensed the exhaustion and his readiness to be left alone. I instructed my nephew that we turn the device off. As we were leaving, we had a couple of final questions as we thanked Henry for the information provided by him.

We asked if a child was present in the house, and if so, what happened to her in her physical life: It stated the following:

Autumn

Growing

Death

We interpreted that her Native American name was Autumn, growing meaning that she was a child, and "death" obviously that she had, in fact, died.

Moving forward again to the paranormal session. None of our findings were revealed to them until after the session. We wanted to compare notes after their session. We all entered the house at first, and immediately the television set "turned on by itself!" It's ways of letting us know of its presence. Those of us who were not part of the paranormal group were instructed to view via the monitor rather than be in the potentially "unsafe" dwelling.

In fact, they discovered through the first portion that the main spirits name was in fact "Henry"! They (the paranormal team) were finding out information on the other five ghosts, and why they would not move on. Henry prevented it their moving on, somehow, and thus they were stuck in limbo. His purpose in keeping them hostage was to feed off of their energy. Without them, he would indeed go dormant.

At this point, I had reached my maximal tolerance. I was becoming overwhelmed at the details of the haunting. I left for about an hour, and when I returned, the ordained priest walked to my car and informed me that the five spirits had moved on to the light (A happy yet eerie feeling. I sensed progress was being made).

He stated, furthermore, that the main ghost, Henry, was refusing to move on.

The second half of the session began. It was approaching 10:00 PM, and the goal was for each paranormal team member to be settled, near a bed, a chair, or something similar. As they became settled, shadows began to transpire, images were showing face, orbs were more active, and a clear voice could be heard in the office. In a very low voice, it stated, "IIIIIIIImmmm. It sounded firm, very firm. It must have been Henry.

Several photos revealed ghosts which were so clear that anyone could spot them without having to have them pointed out. A child, a dark-headed woman, a shadow-ghost (camouflaging itself on the woodwork in the main hallway, and a clear image against the headboard of the bed.) Other, less vivid ghosts were in the photographs, but these stuck out clearly.

Finally, after exhaustingly dealing with "Henry" they noticed his energy was waning quickly, partly because of the passing of the other five ghosts, and partially from exhaustion.

The paranormal's had completed their mission and explained that the house was clean. I asked about the vestige of Henry, and they explained that his source of energy was removed and he would eventually go dormant (even with my brother there! Which meant, the house was inhabitable, even for my brother!) What a relief. One of the team members was still inside, insisting that Henry leave "Autumn" alone as she was on the other side! Our little radar had picked up on some major stuff and coincided with some of their findings!

One of the team members insisted on viewing the device and told the leader, who was surprised as well, about the findings. Unfortunately, it was not admissible evidence at this point.

Since the groups cleaning, my brother's house has the "warmth" that was present when we viewed the house. I sense nothing now, and my brother is, at long last, improving health-wise.

I've spent some time alone, of which I would have been disturbed by the spirits. Not even a thought of them entered my mind!

His home is lovely and warm again, and I thank the society for their hard work. They do not charge a fee, but take donations. This type of deal, for me, is worth much indeed. After all, it can determine life or death on some level. God Bless Our Happy Home... and those who made it possible. ∎

Volume 3: Ghost Stories from Texas

Murdered Souls
Woden, Texas

We moved into this house a bit over 4 years ago. It's a huge brick, very nice, well made home. It has its flaws like most older homes do. It creaks, and most doors are falling off, but nothing we can't fix ourselves.

It all started about 3 months after we moved in. My husband, myself and our two children, oh and Fifi our cat. I remember sitting alone in the living room while the children were at school. I was watching General Hospital. When a commercial came on I heard walking above me. So I turned the TV all the way down to listen. As I did I heard a man talking. "What in the world?" I jumped up off the couch and headed outside to see if maybe someone was on the roof working or something! And there was no one!

I sat back down thinking I was losing my mind. All of the sudden I heard him again. And it sounded as he was tapping his foot to a beat! I immediately called my husband. He said he would be right there. When he got home nearly 20 minutes later the noise had already stopped. But I made him check anyway. He went up to the attic, but no one was there! He thought I was crazy.

Later that night I had gotten the kids ready for bed and sent them to their rooms. I turned off the kitchen light and grabbed a blanket from the chair and headed to the couch where I was going to relax and watch a movie, but before I sat down I noticed a huge green circular glow on the wall near the hallway, about three feet tall! Freaked out, I went straight to bed and held my husband for comfort!

A few months later I was cleaning the kitchen adjacent to the office. Finishing up the kitchen, I went to shut the doors to the office. It's two small doors with very small magnets at the top to keep the doors shut.

The doors opened back up with full force. I grabbed the doors to attempt to shut them again, but I felt a strong force pulling them open. Finally shutting them, they flew open again. I asked my oldest son, who was 9 at the time, to come see what was going on. He tried to shut them but again it was forced open, and we both freaked out and left the doors standing open!

As my husband came home, we had him try to shut the door. And of course it did. He thought I was crazy, but I had my son as a witness! The doors to this day will open by themselves. And my husband has experienced the force.

I had to move my daughter out of her room. She would not sleep in it at all. Our cat Fifi was always hiding somewhere, and could never find her.

I remember the scariest days so clearly. We would all be in the living room watching TV or even just playing a game, and the dryer would just start on its own!

After all of these ongoing experiences we asked around a lot.

We found out that two people had been murdered in this house nearly 10 years ago on Valentine's Day. It was a husband and wife.

The wife's brother is the one that shot them both. He told his girlfriend what he did that same day, then shot her and himself! He is in prison and the girlfriend lived.

We are so used to weird things occurring that it doesn't bother us anymore. But we are in the market for a new house, and can't wait to start over peacefully! The couple was buried nearly 3 miles down the road. And I hope they will both find peace. ■

Die. Just... Die.
Fort Worth, Texas

Recently I figured out that I can make a really weird noise with my knuckles and my elbow. In cheerleading we would do a move where we would put one arm bent across our chests horizontally, then we'd snap our arms downward to a vertical position, and then pump our fists in the air. Well, when I do that, it sounds like I'm dead or a zombie from my bones popping. In addition to that, when I crack my knuckles it sounds like a horse running.

So, anyway, one night I was with my friend upstairs in her bedroom, and she wanted to hear the noise I can make with my elbow. As soon as I did that, I heard a voice say, "Die."

I asked her if she said that, or if perhaps her brother was playing tricks. We checked around and her brother wasn't even home. So, we just forgot about it for the time being. She began practicing it herself, trying to imitate the sound with her own elbow. When she was really close to doing it right, we again heard the words, "Just die." We were scared to death!

We ran down the hall into her parents' room. Her mom's favorite show was on (The Real Housewives of Orange County), but her dad was willing to come with us to check it out. We told him we heard the words, "Die. Just die" whenever we did the cheer move.

He said, "Alright. Let me see it." We both did it at the same time, and this time the voice spoke the complete phrase, "Die. Just die. DIE!"

we ran into him to hug him for protection. He was concerned enough to begin setting up an air mattress to let us sleep on the floor in his room with her mom. Her mom asked us, "why are you girls in here?" We explained it her, and she wanted to hear it herself.

We quickly did the move three times for her. The first time, the voice simply said, "die." The second time we did it, the voice said, "Just die." The third time we did it, the voice said, "Die. Just die. DIE!" At that point we heard her dad yell for us, and we ran out of the room. We were already crying when we ran to him.

He tried it himself, and he could do it too, but we heard something a little different. He did the move and there was laughing. Then he did it again and there was a creak in the floor. He did it one last time, and the bathroom mirror shattered!

We all went to bed downstairs, sleeping on the floor and the couches. Not even her parents were about to stay upstairs after that.

My Grave
Denison, Texas

I live next door to an eerie graveyard. My bedroom is on the bottom floor in the back of my house, so I can look right out my window and see the graveyard. It's very spooky.

One night a few years ago, I was taking a walk around the graveyard after my parents had gone to bed. Graveyards are so quiet and peaceful, and I love them. I saw a little boy walking down the road coming towards me. At first I just thought that it was a neighbor boy. He was wearing a suit and his hair was all nice and it looked like he just got out of church.

He stopped in front of a grave and pointed at it. He then looked up at me and just stood there for a few moments pointing at the grave.

Just as I was beginning to feel real creeped out, he mouthed, "Me". Then he just vanished.

I was scared senseless. The next day, after I regained my senses, I went to the grave and read the marker. It was the final resting place of a little boy. ∎

The Girl in my Hallway
Houston, Texas

It was Christmas day. As a matter of fact, around 3a.m. As most kids do, I was sneaking out of my room to look under the tree, in hopes that Santa Clause had brought me what I wanted that year. My house had a completely straight hallway that led into the living room. My room was at the very end of the hallway.

I carefully and as quietly as I could, walked out of my room. From right outside my bedroom door I could see someone run from our Christmas tree into the kitchen which was right off the living room. I specifically remember seeing brown hair whip around the corner so I was sure it was a girl.

At the time, I figured it was my little sister who was also checking her presents, and thought it was our parents, so she ran and hid. That was, until something else happened.

It was about two years until I had another sighting. It was about the same time (3 a.m.). I was extremely sick with the flu and couldn't go to sleep whatsoever, so I was wide awake. I left my room and went down the hallway toward the bathroom, being quiet hoping not to wake anyone up.

There was a small laundry chute that had once led into the laundry room, but after remodeling our house it now just led into a wall. I was about two feet from the chute when, as nonchalantly as anything...

A girl glided through my wall and halted right in front of where I was standing. She cocked her head in an inhuman position and looked at me.

I could tell her eyes were staring into mine, but it was as if she was looking right through me. I was petrified.

I tried to scream but it was like the saying says, "cat got your tongue?" Then as if I wasn't even there, she proceeded into the laundry chute, floating directly through the wall.

I was traumatized after that occurrence, so I convinced my parents to get a priest to come and perform an exorcism on our house. The priest came and did the routine. I was hiding in my room, half expecting an explosion of some sort. But nothing happened. My parents as well as the priest were convinced I had had a dream or pulled a prank, but I knew.

That night I was awoke by distraught noises. A girl's scream for sure. It was like the sound of a cat being stretched and pulled causing it to wail and hiss altogether. I've never since heard a sound so horrifying.

The noise was followed by a barrage of flying objects and crashes which never resulted in broken objects. My door creaked open. I sunk into my bed. I began to cry hysterically and curled up into a ball.

When the hallway was fully visible, a pair of red, demonic-like eyes seemed to float into my room. It drifted into the far wall and disappeared.

That was about a month ago. Ever since then I have had strange experiences with the paranormal. Just yesterday I opened my closet door and saw a little girl hanging from the clothes rack, with her eyes gouged out. I'm completely terrified, I'm not sure what to do. As far as I know, no one else in our house has seen these apparitions. I can't sleep at night and nobody will believe me.

The ghost has yet to pose a threat but I'm finding it very difficult to live in this house. ■

The Bloody Little Boy
Wimberly, Texas

If you've read my story "Back and Forth..." you know about the horrible things that go on at my house. This event, however, takes place at my friend Frank's house.

It was late May and Frank was throwing a big party to celebrate the end of the school year at his house in Wimberly. Everybody was having a great time at the party enjoying the beginning of summer. At about 11:30 p.m.,

Frank sent everybody home except me and a few of his closest friends. We were up until 3:00 when we passed out. Everybody was asleep in the living room except me and frank who fell asleep while we were talking in his room.

I'm not sure what time I woke up but I'm guessing it was around 4:30. I looked around the room trying to remember where I was. In the midst of the darkness there was a bright white light. It was blindingly bright. When my eyes finally adjusted I was able to see that the light was coming from Frank's dresser. I leaned forward to get a better look at whatever was causing the light. I will never forget what I saw.

The light was coming from a picture frame. In the frame was the photo of a young boy with ink black hair. What surprised me most about this picture was his skin. It was an amazingly pale shade of white. I would say he was albino but that was impossible considering the color of his hair. Then I looked at his eyes. They were completely black! The photo was beginning to scare me. That's when I noticed his mouth. It was wide open like he was screaming and his teeth...they were covered in blood!

By then I was so scared that I laid back down on the floor and closed my eyes, refusing to open them until morning came. As soon as the sun came up, I woke up Frank.

"Frank, what is wrong with you?! You sick freak!" I screamed at him.

"What are you talking about?" he yawned back at me.

"Why do you have a horrible picture of a bloody albino boy on your dresser?" I asked.

"What?" He looked at me like I was a lunatic.

At this point my friend Alex walked in. "What are you yelling about?" he asked.

"Frank has a disgusting picture of a bloody albino boy on his dresser! Look!" I pointed to the picture frame and was shocked. The frame now contained a picture of Frank's dog.

Nobody believed my story about the changing photo. They all told me it was just a dream. As the day went on and rational thinking set in I began to believe them. By the time I got home I was laughing at myself for being so stupid.

Later that night I was brushing my teeth getting ready for bed. I opened the medicine cabinet to put the toothpaste away and when I closed it and looked into the mirror, in true cliché fashion, I saw the bloody little boy standing behind me. I nearly chucked on my toothbrush. I stared in the mirror for what seemed like an eternity. Then he spoke to me.

"I found you" he said to me. His voice was indescribable. Every word sent chills down my spine. As he said the last word I finally found the strength to spin around. Of course when I did he was no longer there. A feeling if dread and nausea overwhelmed me. After throwing up, I went to my bed and laid down still trying to understand what just happened. I still don't believe it.

The image of that boy will always haunt me and I feel sick every time I think about him. I've been debating over the past few months on whether or not to post this and finally decided to. I hope you've enjoyed my story.

The Wal-Mart Ghost
Spring, Texas

I went to our local Wal-Mart located on Louetta and I45N in Spring, Texas, to do my weekly shopping. I went to the aisle which has facial tissue, and saw a lot of boxes off the shelf and on the floor. I would say approximately 100 boxes.

I thought to myself, some little kid wiped off the shelves while shopping with their mother. I approached the shelf to reach and get two boxes of tissues when I felt something hit my right leg. I thought the stockers didn't stock the shelves correctly and they were falling off the shelf.

I left that aisle and told Julia, my exchange student from Germany, to wait by the children's department so I could run down the other aisle for laundry soap, bleach, and fabric softener.

As I was coming out of that aisle I could hear something falling on the floor. I looked and it was the tissue aisle again; however it wasn't children pushing them off... I saw an arm which looked like it was coming from behind the shelf make one hard push and lots of boxes of tissues came off the shelf.

Another box began to spin in circles for about 20 seconds, several other boxes were flying off the shelf too. I stood in awe.

Another customer was about 5 feet behind me, and he saw the same thing. I asked him are you seeing what I am seeing? An older lady came out from the infant department and was looking that way, and all three of us stood and looked in amazement.

I called for Julia to see what I was seeing, but by the time she reached it stopped. I told her about it and about the arm, and I looked in the aisle next to it thinking there has to be a reasonable explanation, like someone reached through the other side and pushed them off.

What I saw was a metal backing to the shelf which proved to me that no one could put their hand through from the other side. I told the checkout girl who said that's scary.

When I got home I told my husband, and he told me I should call Wal-Mart and report it. I called and spoke with the assistant manager Jim and told him I was hoping he didn't think I was crazy. He told me they were wondering what happened in that aisle. I asked if they had cameras, he said yes. I asked him if he could view that aisle, he said yes and I asked if I could call to find out the results. He told me to call the next evening. When I did, he said the home office had taken the tape and told him not to talk further about it. He couldn't tell me what was on the tape. ■

Demon With My Face
Abilene, Texas

My story begins two years back on a chilly December night. I was hosting my annual "Cookies and Caroling" party, and the party was finally dwindling down to an end. Early parents were arriving, and only five guests were left along with my cousin, Hilda.

We were all gathered in my room telling ghost stories with all the lights out, and only a flashlight to illuminate our faces. If you live in Texas as I do, you know it never gets below zero most the time and you only need a light jacket to go outside in the winter... it was one of those nights. Bailey and Kyleigh, two of my very close friends, were getting quite restless after a few stories and were ready to do something else.

Bailey announced she was going outside. I reminded her as she walked out not to forget her jacket. Kyleigh and Hilda tagged along, grabbing their jackets as well.

Kristian and Brooke, two of my best friends in the whole world, and myself were still sprawled on the bed, Kristian holding the flashlight and a book in my lap.

About five minutes later I heard screaming, a door slamming, and my mom saying, "Quiet down!"

Bailey, Kyleigh, and Hilda pushed through my doorway gasping. Then they saw me and their mouths dropped open really, really wide.

"But you, you, you.. were outside, but you're not and..." they all stammered.

"Tell me the story," was all I had to say, and they started to spill. This is what they said:

They were walking outside when they swear they saw me in the corner of my yard (I had a big yard so it was hard to see from one corner to the other when it's dark). They said it was crouching and "my" long hair was covering "my" face.

Bailey asked, "You okay, Maddy?" Of course it didn't answer. Then they all started calling out my name.

When it didn't answer again, Kyleigh said, "That's not Maddy." Then they ran in.

I know this story is true, because later after everyone was gone, Kristian, Brooke, and I went back outside and sat on the swing set. After only a few minutes we heard footsteps. We turned around and there this thing was, smiling. Yes it did look like me, only with black skin and bright red eyes. We, too, screamed and ran for our lives into my house. ◼

Ghost House
Buda, Texas

I lived in California until I had to move with my family when we couldn't afford our house anymore. We moved to Texas. The new house was old, and very big. I wanted to cry, I hated that house so much. Especially one particular night.

That night, while I was sleeping, I woke up to hearing a baby crying. Unfortunately, we don't have a baby. I got up, half asleep, and ran to tell my parents. They got up and went into the empty room where I heard the crying. They didn't see or hear anything. I went back to bed, scared and shocked.

Then the crying started again. I didn't move. For what felt like an hour the crying didn't stop! I was so tired, suddenly out of nowhere I said, "Shut up!" That was the worst thing I could have done. About 5 seconds later, I heard a woman sobbing. Then she screamed "No! Don't please!" then a shot fired.

I couldn't move. I wanted to scream but nothing came out. Then the baby started crying again. Another shot fired, then silence. I started to cry. I wanted to puke. Then, my door creaked open. I stopped breathing. A lump crawled across the room. It groaned. I screamed and I ran as fast as I could to get out of there.

I ran to my parents room and woke my mother and I told her I'm sleeping here. The next morning I went to my room and found nothing there. I went to the empty room and found nothing also.

I got on the computer and looked up info on the house. As it turns out, this house belonged to a man named Richard and his wife Anna. They had a baby named Richard, Jr. The husband killed both of them and then himself. The wife had managed to crawl out if the other room to the next room down. She died before she could reach the phone. That would have been my room. ■

Back and Forth...
Lockhart, Texas

Let me start off by saying that this story is 100% true. Nobody believes me when I tell this story, but I promise this is true.

Just about two months after my fifth birthday, my father died. On his birthday the very next year, the two light fixtures in my kitchen fell simultaneously at exactly midnight. This was only the beginning of my haunting.

Not much else happened until I was about eight and my step-dad moved in. Around this time I began to notice shadows moving when there was no light or people to cause them. When I told my mom she brushed it off as me not handling my step-dad moving in well.

It only got worse as the years went by when I began hearing voices, whispers, and footsteps in the dead of night.

The first time my mom left me alone at the house I heard footsteps going up and down the hall! I was all alone and at this time we had no pets.

That very night I woke up to go to the bathroom and as I was walking into the bathroom I heard a deep voice say, "You'd better not." I spun around and saw nothing. I turned on the bathroom light and a shampoo bottle which had been in the tub fell to the floor as if from the ceiling! I ran back to my room terrified and I heard a woman's voice (which was not my mother's) shout, "What are you doing?!" I hid under my covers for the rest of the night.

Also on several occasions my sister's bedroom light would turn on at night when she was at friends' houses. One night when I was asleep I heard whispering in my room and the light turned on by itself. The scariest part of this is that I was watching the light switch turn on by itself.

The scariest of these events just happened about a year ago. For Christmas a few years ago my aunt gave me this amazing clock that would beep and light up when it sensed motion. It would also rock back and forth on its stand. I loved that clock, until about a year ago when the most terrifying experience of my life happened.

One thing you should know about the clock is that it is extremely sensitive and will often beep and light up when the house settles so it's not strange to hear it go off at random times.

Well one night about a year ago I was lying in bed, unable to sleep. I heard my clock go off by itself which I brushed off as the house settling which it did quite often. About a minute after it beeped the first time, it beeped a second time, and then a third. I turned over to face the desk on which the clock was lying and was horrified. The clock kept beeping over and over again as if someone was walking past it over an over again or waving their hand in front of it. I listened in horror as it beeped by itself at least 20 more times. *Beep beep* over and over again in a terrifying melody. Not only beeping, it was rocking back and forth on its stand! I just laid there hypnotized and frozen in fear. Suddenly after about two minutes, it just stopped. I buried my face in my pillow and cried out of fright.

The incidents at my house just keep getting scarier. Almost every night I hear whispering and footsteps outside of my door. I'll be happy when I finally move out in a few years and get away from this horrible place!

Thirsty Ghost
Corpus Christi, Texas

About ten years ago, my mother lived in a very old house that was kind of secluded. We were not sure of the exact age, but it was built before the turn of the century.

This house was two stories, and had a strange layout. On the upper level, there was what looked like a hidden door. One day my sister and I were exploring, and decided to look behind this small door. We found a narrow stairway that looked like it used to go down stairs, but had been closed up.

There was still a remaining portion of the stairway leading up, and we followed it. This was a very weak and unstable set of stairs, which only had eight or so steps. It lead to yet another door, which opened to a long, narrow compartment. This compartment went in a circular pattern around the attic space. There were about three small makeshift doors throughout the compartment. We had no idea what it was for. My mother suggested maybe it was for storage.

This house had always given me the creeps. I felt that something was wrong with it, and with the land on which it sat. The owner had bought the house, for what was owed in taxes, from the city. It had been vacant for some time, and he wanted to rent it out so that kids would quit partying out there.

My mother felt drawn to the house; she said it had a feeling of timelessness. I thought it was just an old, ugly house that needed to be torn down. My mother had made a lot of repairs, which were needed.

While cutting down the high grown weeds in back, my mother and brother found three mounds and what looked like remnants of old wooden crosses. At first, she thought nothing of it, as there were a lot of strange things about this land and the house.

One strange thing was the addition that was added on and never quite finished; it was as if someone built it just to take up space. There were no finishings, only the floor, ceiling, and walls, and no plugs or outlets. This was odd, because you could tell that it was a recent addition, and there were outlets throughout the rest of the house. I never could go into that room. Every time I tried, I couldn't breathe and I felt that something dark was in there. My brother made the room into his hangout room. No matter how much light was in there, it always seemed dark.

My brother suddenly quit going in there, and locked the door. He never said why, he just wouldn't go near there. That was about the time that things got active. There was always a feeling of unease there, along with the toilet that would flush by itself, the faucets that would run without being turned on, and the unidentifiable noises.

One day, my little sister came running inside screaming. After we got her to calm down, all she said was, "She's dead." My brother went to investigate what she was talking about, and outside, not too far from the house, he yelled and kicked something.

When we went outside, we found her cat had been decapitated. We thought that someone had done it to be hateful, but didn't know who would do such a thing.

Later that night, my sister heard a man talking outside her window. She couldn't make out what was said, and when we searched, no one was found.

Then everything seemed quiet for a while. Until one day, while my mother was doing dishes, she heard a little boy. She had heard his voice several times, but never saw him. He would always say, "Momma, I'm thirsty". At first, she thought it was my brother, and would tell him to get a drink. After realizing that no one was there, she finally came to ignore the voice.

On this day, she not only heard him, but also heard the voice of a woman. My mother looked out the kitchen door, and there they stood. A little black boy, and what we think was his mother. He was crying and asking his mother for a drink while she was trying to pull him away, saying to him to be quiet or the master would beat him again.

My mother was a woman who accepted the presence of spirits, so she was not too alarmed by this. She simply said that the boy could come in and have a drink. The woman said, "thank you ma'am," and they disappeared. That is the only time she has seen them. After that encounter, the faucets quit coming on by themselves. There still was the presence that we can only describe as a hate-filled man.

Shortly after a horrible experience, my mother moved out. About a month after moving, the house fell in. It is not understood why.

I think it was probably vandals. But my mother believed otherwise. She also began to believe that those mounds in the back were graves. Possibly of the little boy and his mother.

When checking around about the property, we learned that the original owner had been a slave owner who had treated his slaves badly. He would force them to go without food or water for long periods of time. This led us to believe, although it is not documented, that the little boy and his mother died due to this man's cruelty. We never did find out who or what killed my sister's cat. I try never to drive down that road where the house stood. I always get an eerie feeling whenever I pass the property. ■

Three Bridges
Edgewood, Texas

There are so many stories of ghost encounters near or at the Three Bridges. My encounter is near it.

Me and my two friends decided to go walking and it was already pretty late. The reason we did, I don't know? Lucy is a chicken, she was so scared of walking at night. So being the nice guy I am, acted like I saw someone in the woods by the road and they took off running, but stopped about 200 yards ahead of me watching me. I was just standing still looking in the woods, then I jumped back (I was at the edge of the road so when I jumped back I jumped in the trees, and I ran to the edge and came out, deciding joke's over.) So I looked down the road and there were Lucy and Emily walking in the opposite direction. I ran up to them and they stopped and looked at me.

Their eyes, I don't know how to explain what they looked like, if that makes any sense, but what scared me the most was the smiles on their faces. It was not normal, they were demonic looking, and then I heard someone calling my name. I looked behind me to find Lucy and Emily looking in the woods and shouting my name. I looked back and no one was there with me.

To this day I don't know what I saw, but I have never played a trick like that again, and I still feel like I'm being watched every where I go. ■

The Lying Ouija Board
San Antonio, Texas

When my oldest daughter was fifteen and we were stationed on a base in Sembach Germany, I had the weirdest dream. I dreamt of us moving back to the U.S. into a dark, creepy looking house. As the dream progressed I saw different things. I saw myself trying to clean the house and crying because no matter how hard I tried I couldn't get it clean. Then I saw a strange plaid jacket hanging on the coat tree in the foyer that had those old fashioned mirror tiles on the wall that reflected whoever came to the front door. The next part was the worst, with someone breaking in. I could hear them rummaging around in the other rooms and I was hiding in my bathroom. Suddenly they were trying to cut through the wall with a chainsaw. These people wanted to kill us. I knew it in my heart, but didn't know why. I realized the jacket I had seen earlier was my husband's and that it being there on the coat tree meant he was gone on military duty somewhere. He always left it there when he was gone.

So in the dream I finally knew that I was alone in the house, the kids were at a bunking party at the youth center on base. As the intruders were sawing through the wall I managed to get out a sliding window and jumped onto a rooftop made up of tar and gravel. I jumped onto the pecan tree next to the roof and fell from its branches to the ground. Then I started running from the yard, and as I got to the corner of the front yard I saw the intruders coming after me. They ran under the low hanging limbs of a weeping willow tree.

From all that happened in this dream, I knew it was a premonition dream. I've had premonition dreams my whole life, and I'm 55 years old.

I told my teenage daughter about it and we both agreed that we would recognize the house in my dream and make sure we didn't move into it. But we had to return to the States early due to my son having a mental illness called schizophrenia, that required him to be in a children's psychiatric hospital.

We stayed on base in guest housing for over a month and then moved into a really nice house, nothing like the dream house (or should I say nightmare?). We had applied to buy the house but it failed the VA inspection so we couldn't get a loan. We were really in dire need of a new place to live since the owner gave us 30 days to move and we had to let prospective buyers in all the time. I was working nights and it was getting irritating to have to wake up, get dressed, and show the house, or answer the phone and talk to the realtor and arrange appointments. Try 30 days of strangers in and out at odd hours and you'd be in a rush to get out, too.

A friend of mine had a friend who worked in rentals at Century 21 and she took us to see a lot of places. However, the nice ones were too expensive or too far from the base. We finally got a decent place and by this time that dream was the furthest thing from my mind.

Regardless, this house started to make itself known. First I saw the coat on the coat tree exactly like the dream, and my husband was off in Turkey. So I took down the coat tree and boxed it up with yard sale stuff. Next I noticed how dark the dining room and den were with dark brown paneling, so I got some wallpaper to hang to lighten it up.

Then our cook stove was full of grease from previous renters cooking on the griddle in the center and just letting the grease run into the rest of the stove as the drip pan was missing. So I tried and tried to get it clean, even dismantling it and soaking the parts in the bathtub. The main problem wasn't so much the grease, but every time I turned it on bugs came running out. I guess they lived in it because of the grease buildup. I cried and cried and finally got my oldest daughter's boyfriend to take the whole stove outside into the back yard. When he came in he mentioned there were a lot of pecans on the tree in the back yard. I hadn't known there was one back there.

So many clues we missed. Then my daughter and her friends started messing around with an Ouija board. She came into my bedroom one night and crouched down by the side of my bed and with tears in her eyes said she had some bad news for me. When I asked her what it was she said that my youngest brother Billy came through on the Ouija board and said he had died of a drug overdose.

Billy had been missing a few years, but he was over 21 and could go where he wanted and wasn't legally obligated to inform anyone. Well I got angry and told her to stay away from that board because it would lie like that to get a toehold in her life. I told her I would prove it to her by praying to the Good Lord about it to find out the truth. That next night Billy called from Florida where he had spent the last year in jail and wanted to know if he could come stay with us. He had a ride with a trucker that would bring him all the way to San Antonio.

I proved that Ouija wrong, but I still did not recognize the danger we would soon all face.

Almost every thing I saw in that dream was true about that house. Even one night when someone climbed in through the window of the room my brother slept in. The guy said he was looking for my teenaged daughter Becky. Which that used to be her room until we found out she was sneaking out. So we changed her to a room with burglar bars. The only room that did, actually. Evidently she had been sneaking people in as well.

The last straw for that house came when the first time we all left the house together to go out to eat. At the time we had 8 people in the house.

Someone tried to bust into the back door. It had a hasp and padlock on it and it was just our luck to come home and see someone running from the corner of the yard past the low hung branches of the weeping willow tree.

Note: we also found out that the previous owner had died in a car accident just down the road. It happened a few days after he finished building the den with fireplace and wet bar onto the back of the house and the roof was made of tar and gravel.

We used to hear a sound like someone walking around on

that roof and sounds like somebody doing carpentry work. That was before the next door lady told me about the owner dying.

I talked out loud to his spirit one time and told him as long as I lived there I would fix things. After that the odd sounds went away. I think he was the reason that whoever tried to break the back door open was not able to, because the screws were almost out of the door jamb and it seemed like one good yank would have pulled that door right open.

I just say thank you to whoever was watching over us until we could get a new house.

Angry Motel Ghost
Temple, Texas

My father-in-law passed away just days after Thanksgiving in 1992. When he was diagnosed with cancer, the doctors said he had less than a year. It came as no surprise, as both my husband's parents were heavy smokers. He smoked big old cigars, and she smoked at least two packs of cigarettes a day.

We live in Texas, but most of our relatives live in Arkansas, so I told my mother-in-law that if she needed her son, to call and I would make sure he got leave from his Air Force job to go help her. Plus I wanted him to spend those last days with his father. I knew what it was like to lose someone and not be able to say goodbye. My uncle that raised me died when we were stationed in Germany and it was hard on me. I didn't want my husband to go through that.

My mother-in-law called and told me her husband had fallen from the hospital bed they set up in their den. She wasn't able to get him back in the bed and she couldn't get ahold of anybody, so he had to lay there for hours. I called my husband at work and told him he needed to go help his parents, now. He got the next flight out.

I drove down for the funeral, spent a few days with family, and then he and I drove back home to Texas.

After the funeral my mother-in-law loaded our station wagon with things she wanted my husband to have that belonged to his Dad. They were also clearing out her house so she could move closer to her daughter. We had one of those big old Brady Bunch station wagons, the kind with wood grain on the sides. Or as my husband called it, an "Uncle Buck-mobile" after the John Candy movie.

We made good time going back home until we got just past Waco. Then the station wagon started acting up. The engine started backfiring and fire would shoot out from the tailpipe . It was like the motor had hiccups. Well, about an hour into this the engine backfired one last time and shut down. We had been driving through freezing rain for the last two hours, and when the motor quit it didn't take long for the heat to dissipate.

By chance, some guys in a wrecker came by and worked on the engine. They charged us a hundred dollars, the last of our cash. We got going again and not more than 10 miles down the road and BANG!! The engine backfired again. Fire billowed out the tailpipe, and we pulled off the road once again. My husband got out, raised the hood, fiddled with something, and then hollered for me to turn the key on. This time a little flame shot up and scared the wits out of me. Finally it started again. But 10 minutes later, Kablooey! Another half an hour's wait.

We continued to just drive in these ten-minute increments. We finally saw a LaQuinta motel and slowly limped the wagon into the parking lot. My husband rented us a room and I was relieved to be out of the freezing cold.

By now the roads were getting near impossible. Ice was everywhere.

The room had two twin beds, but I didn't care, I just climbed under the covers and conked out. I was sawing some serious zzz's, when suddenly I couldn't breathe. I thought I was having a panic attack, which I get from time to time. Considering the circumstances I wouldn't have been surprised to have one now. I tried to get up to get a glass of water from the bathroom. I was thinking that maybe the heater was on too high, as causing me to choke.

Just as I started to sit up, I felt myself slammed back onto the mattress. Again I tried to rise and couldn't move. Only now I could feel something holding my wrists above my head.

I was struggling just to get a breath of air because whatever was happening, it was putting pressure on my chest. It felt like something was pressed over my nose and mouth. This was no panic attack! Something was on me. Then I felt whatever it was trying to actually enter my body.

That was the most awful feeling I have ever had in my life. It was like this force wanted to take over my body and push me out. And there wasn't enough room for two people in one body. I've had a spinal myleogram and when they inject die into your spine it starts feeling like a pressure like when your ears pop in changing elevation, but ten times worse. This felt a hundred times stronger. I kept pushing against whatever was holding me down and finally I gritted my teeth, and pushed up with all my might and coughed out,

"Get off of me!"

My husband was snoring away in the other bed and I hoarsely called his name. I was still short of breath, so I scrambled off the bed I was on and climbed in on the other side of his bed. My husband woke up and held me until I calmed down. Then he got up to get me a glass of water from the bathroom and when he turned on the light I could see a swirling black mass above the bed I had been in. I yelled at my husband to look and he saw the same thing. My heart is pounding right now as I am recalling that night.

The mass got thicker and darker and started moving towards my husband. I was terrified. I didn't know what this thing was, but I could feel emotions in the air.

Thick sadness, grief, anger, revenge, all those emotions were settling onto me and I suddenly realized that someone had been strangled to death on that bed. I could feel that the presence was male and more than any other emotion, anger was the strongest. This presence was extremely angry. It wanted whoever else came into it's aura to know it was mad.

I shouted to my husband to come back to the bed and leave the lights on. The presence seemed to be confined to that second bed. Right now I was ready to go back to the station wagon, freezing cold or not. I wanted so much to be home. My husband pulled aside the heavy curtains on the window and thankfully it was now daylight.

We went to the lobby and ate breakfast and we managed to get a tow truck to take our vehicle and us home,

I have no idea what happened in that motel room but I do know this, I will never stay there again.

The Church, the Priest, and My Son
Laredo, Texas

In 2002 I ran away from home with a boy my parents did not approve of. I was 18 at the time (and pregnant). My boyfriend, Johnny, was almost 21. We stayed at a friend's house for about a week then started house hunting. I was broke but Johnny had a small amount of money coming in from his extremely supportive parents.

The first two houses we looked at were perfect, but extremely out of our price range. When we drove up to the third house, I automatically noticed the cross on the roof. The real estate agent began telling us about it.

It was a small abandoned church. The outside was messy with twigs and dead plants everywhere, but the inside was beautiful. Wood floors, and pretty red carpeted stairs to a second floor. I walked up the stairs while Johnny talked with Todd, the real estate agent. I immediately got a bad feeling.

There were only two rooms. I walked into the first and saw crosses everywhere. On the walls, painted on the floor and even hanging from the fan. I shut the door quickly and went to room number two. This one was completely empty except for a Roman Gothic window which was open. This room gave me chills too. Johnny came up and stood behind me, he looked and said it would be a perfect room for the baby.

He walked to the other room and looked. The crosses didn't bother him. He said we could remove them all. I said nothing and walked back downstairs. I walked through the small kitchen and to the potential living room. There were two pews and a statue of the Virgin Mary with baby Jesus. I told Johnny I didn't like it and I wasn't going to live there. He told me it was in our price range and perfect. Reluctantly I agreed.

A week later we moved in. Everything was normal until the first night. I was upstairs trying to remove the crosses when I heard Johnny calling me from downstairs. I yelled back at him telling him I was busy. "Dani! Dani! Danica! Get down here now!" he yelled, sounding scared and angry. I went down and he started yelling at me telling me how I wasn't funny and that I need to stop playing childish pranks on him. I had no idea what he was talking about. He told me that he saw a Rosary lift off the statue of Mary and into the air then drop again. I got very nervous after that.

We removed everything. The pews, the crosses, we took it all out and gave it to a local church. Everything seemed normal after that.

About a month after that I had the baby. We named him Anthony. We set up his nursery in the room upstairs - the one that had been empty when we moved in.

For the first few months nothing happened. Johnny got a job and was gone a lot of the day at work. I stayed home with Anthony. One day I was downstairs making myself lunch when I heard Anthony cry from upstairs where he was taking a nap. I assumed nothing was wrong as I went up to check on him. When I did he wasn't in his crib. He was sitting on the floor. I called Johnny, and he thought I was losing my mind.

We began fighting a lot when all these incidents would happen. Anthony kept escaping his crib according to Johnny. I knew something was moving him because a baby that is only five months old can't crawl out of his four foot tall crib.

One night I woke up in the chair that I had fallen asleep on with Anthony in my arms. It was the day before Christmas Eve and we were sitting in front of our brightly lit tree. Then I heard something. I turned around to see a priest in black standing there. I thought I was dreaming but then I realized I wasn't when he walked toward me and reached for Anthony. I screamed and Johnny ran downstairs, but he didn't see anything.

The next night, Christmas Eve, we had some friends over. Anthony was sitting with Johnny and we were just talking. Then I saw him again. The priest was standing at the bottom of the steps. I didn't scream this time. Instead I tapped Johnny on the shoulder. He turned and saw him too and jumped up. Then the priest vanished. Our friends thought we were drunk, so they just laughed off Johnny's reaction.

They left a little later and we decided to have Anthony sleep with us that night. We woke up Christmas morning only to find that he was gone. Me and Johnny began panicking and searching for him. We heard him cry from downstairs. We ran down and saw Anthony lying down unharmed on a pile of hay under the Christmas tree. We grabbed him and left the house. We went back a few days later to get our stuff, then we moved out. We never could explain the things that happened or why they happened. We thought the priest had set Anthony up on a pile of hay on Christmas to make it seem like the birth of Jesus Christ.

We never were sure. We tried very hard to forget it.

Now, 8 years later I'm 26 and happily married to Johnny.

And Anthony has grown up to be a happy normal 8 year old. He doesn't remember or know about the church, and we won't ever tell him, but every Christmas Day while Anthony opens his gifts me and Johnny can't help but look back on the incidents that took place in that horrible church. ■

Shawn
Dallas, Texas

When I was younger I used to experience a lot of things in my grandmother's house. When I lived there I used to have a little ghostly friend I would play with named Shawn.

We eventually moved out of my grandfather's house to another house about an hour away. My mom and dad also decided to have more children.

I started school and completely forgot about Shawn. Well when my brother turned about the age I was when I started to see Shawn, he would tell us about it. But it was only when we visited Grandma.

One night at dinner my little brother told us that Shawn wanted his help. I didn't catch on right away, but my mother instantly remembered who Shawn from my experiences with him.. At first we kinda ignored it, until he started getting bruises and scratches on his face and arms when he went over there.

The weird thing is my grandmother didn't have a cat or anything that could make claw marks on his face like that.

The thing that bothered us the most though, before we had the house blessed, is that my brother came to us and told us at the age of four (and I do not know how a four year old would know or come up with this), that Shawn told him he fell in a pool and drowned. He added that his body is under ground and there are bugs crawling in his body. And

Shawn told him that he needed his help to feel better. And, that dying wouldn't hurt my brother. We never let him be by his self in that house ever again.

It gives me chills still thinking about it...

To Grandmother's House I Go
Plano, Texas

Due to the difficult economic times my father lost his job back in '08, forcing my mother and I to move into an apartment complex in Plano, Texas. I was 18 and on my way to college, but the living arrangements had always been a difficult situation. I was able to get in using scholarships, but I still had nowhere to live.

After countless arguments, something changed. My grandmother passed away, leaving me her house near the college I would be attending. It was a mixture of pain for her death and relief on my parents' financial burden.

My grandmother was a very strange woman. She had lived in that house ever since my mom moved out to college. But after her husband (my grandfather) died, she became unstable and was ultimately institutionalized a few years back due to hallucinations of ghosts or spirits or whatever. She lived out her final years back at home, alone.

I remember when I was 7 years old I was staying at her house.

Early in the morning my mom had woken me up, looking terrified and said that we had to leave, and I was forbidden to ever go into that house again.

My mother tried to stop me from moving into that house, but ultimately gave in, knowing that there was no choice. To this day she has never explained to me what happened to her in that house.

This house was just off a dirt path. It was a one story with 3 bedrooms and 2 bathrooms. Toward the end of her life my grandmother had boarded up all of the windows. The house was beautiful; white shutters, a white door, with bricks that seemed to shine under the right light. It was intoxicating. I couldn't understand why my mother wanted me out of it.

The first thing I did was take the boards down. The evening sun shone through the windows making the room dazzle with the reflection of all the colors around the room. I was ready to spend the next 4 years here. I never knew I would only last one week.

I set up my sleeping bag, brushed my teeth and tucked myself in, falling asleep instantly. I woke up around 3 in the morning to scratching on the bathroom floor, and a muffled cry. I ran to the bathroom and swung the door open, no one was inside but there was a pool of blood behind the door, scratch marks on the back of the door, and what looked to be a few teeth. I screamed and ran to call 911. I realized I hadn't hooked up the phones and my cell had died. (How cliché right?)

I went back over to the bathroom to close the door and everything was gone. I froze, not knowing if I was dreaming or crazy. I chalked it up to dreaming. School was started next week, this is when I'm supposed to be relaxing.

The next few nights I slept peacefully but didn't set foot in the bathroom. But the fourth night, I heard it again, louder and more distinct. The moaning turned to a muffled cry, barely audible to understand that this person was crying for help. I knew that voice! It was Grandma's!

I ran to the bathroom and swung the door open and this time I saw her, her legs cuffed to the toilet seat and her hands bound, her mouth gagged. Someone had punched her face because she was bleeding and a tooth had been knocked out. In hysterics I called my mom, she told me to come home immediately.

She explained to me that my grandmother had been murdered and was found chained in her bathroom.

She also explained to me how my grandfather really died, he hung himself and my grandmother relived it over and over. I asked her if that's what she saw when I was younger, she wouldn't answer. I can only guess.

I'll never step foot in my grandmother's house again.

Cell Call

Uvalde, Texas

My step dad had died a couple weeks ago and my mom was praying and asked God if she could see him one more time.

My mom was in the living room with some of her friends. We have a house phone that only relatives are allowed to call on it. The phone started ringing and then it stopped before someone could answer it. The phone is hooked up to our TV so we can check our calls. So my mom checked it and it had my step dad's cell phone number on it and it said his name under the number (Howard). My mom walked to her bedroom freaked out. His cell phone was in a drawer in my moms dresser. She checked it and it was off.

She went back into the living room. When she walked in her friends had turned as white as ghosts. She asked what was wrong. They handed her the phone and it said there was voice message. She brought the phone up to her ear and listened to what it said.

"Darling, I'm ok" said Howard. ■

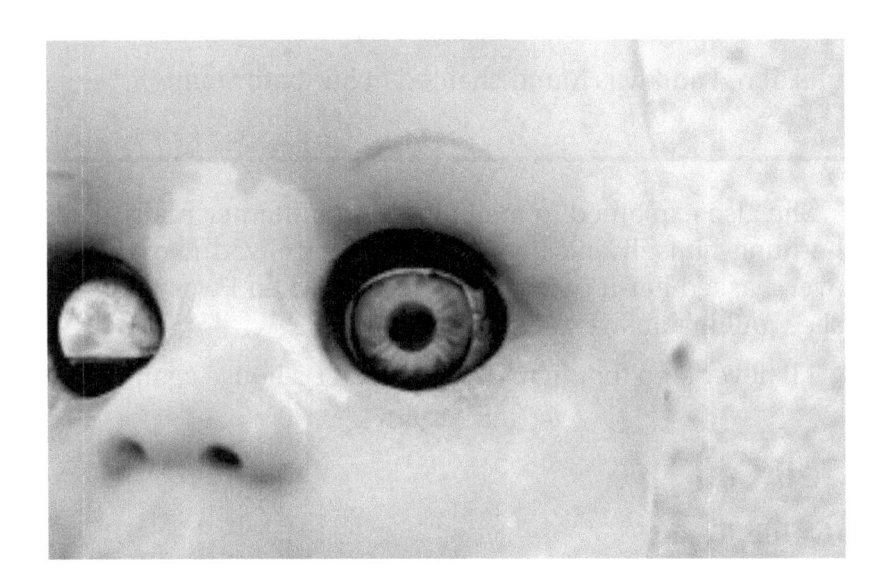

My Doll Shirley
Houston, Texas

When I was a little girl my mother gave me a doll and I named her Shirley. Everything is so clear although it was many years ago.

It was my birthday and we were getting ready to open presents when my mother looked over at my father and nodded. They went to the pantry and pulled out a large box.

It was wrapped in white paper and a pink bow. It was about 3 feet tall.

When I opened it there was a doll. She had blue eyes and long, curly blonde hair. She was wearing a blue dress with a white apron. I thanked my mother I went to play with her outside. That is when things went wrong.

I set her on the swing beside me and ran to go get my mother for a photo. When I ran back outside, my mother following, Shirley was at the top of the slide. Confused, I set her back on the swing and acted like everything was normal.

That same night I was laying in bed with Shirley clutched in my arms. I rolled over to drink some water from the glass on my bedside table. When I rolled back over, she was standing at the end of my bed. I didn't even see or feel her move.

I decided to sleep in the guest room that night. Next week my Aunt and her little girl were coming to visit. We were all laughing and talking in the main room. Where I was sitting, I was facing the door. I saw Shirley peer around the corner. I suddenly got worried because my aunts daughter, Faith, was asleep in the main hall. I excused myself and ran to go get her. I saw Shirley sitting across from her, smiling evilly.

As soon as I brought Faith to my aunt, I snatched up the doll. We had a fire going in the front yard and I got an idea.

I ran to the front yard and tossed her in the fire. First her hair caught flame, then her dress, then her. My mother had been watching and asked me what my deal was. I told her the things that happened and she called my father out, sending me inside.

Curious, I watched from the door. It was very distant but I heard my mother say this one thing very clearly, "I told you we shouldn't have gotten that haunted doll from the dead Man's shop!"

Noises, Voices, Sightings, and Phone Calls
San Antonio, Texas

So we all either believe in ghosts or don't and like to fool with others who do. I did not believe in ghosts until my until one dreadful day.

It was sunny and close to Christmas. Christmas Eve, actually. And I was sitting in my living room watching TV while waiting for the UPS guy to come with my package. My dog was sleeping in my lap and he suddenly jumped up and started barking at the wall.

I walked over to him and said "Sammy, what's wrong?" Even though I knew he could not respond. I looked around and saw nothing. So I picked him up and took him back to the couch with me.

We sat there for about 30 minutes when I got a phone call. I was 13 at the time , so I rarely called anyone or received calls. So this was weird. I picked up my cell phone and looked at the caller ID. It said 'UNKNOWN'. I answered the call just in case it was one of my friends trying to pull a prank on me.

When I answered all I heard was static. Then silence. Then static again. Then I heard a weird, scratchy, male voice on the phone. He sounded distant. Then I heard a high female voice with him. The conversation went like this:

"Oh God no!! Please don't kill me!!"

"Too late woman! You crossed the line! I told you to leave me alone!"

"I'm sorry! I'll go! I'll never come back! Just please don't kill me!"

Then I heard something that sounded like two knives against each other. I heard the woman scream and heels scratching against wood, like she was trying to run away which I imagine she was. Then, as if I hadn't heard enough, there was a gunshot and another scream, which turned into a moan, then a gurgle, then silence. I was about to hang up when I heard the man again.

Except he was closer. Like he was actually holding and talking into the phone. What I heard next chilled me to my very core. He said "Hey there. You like the show? Guess what. You get an encore. You're next." Then the line cut off.

I pressed the end button with a shaking hand. I sat there and tried to shake it off. Easier said than done. I eventually got over it.

After a couple of hours of TV and music I started to hear some strange noises throughout the house.

First I heard scratching and it was not my dog. Second I heard heavy footsteps coming from the second floor. Third I heard banging. Like someone was trying desperately to escape from a room. We do not own a basement but we do have an attic.

Everything was coming from the small door we have in the back of the closet that leads to the attic. I have always been afraid of that door. I never had a good feeling when it came to that door.

I slowly approached it and then I got a cold feeling. Like something went through me. The temperature suddenly dropped and I could see my breath. Then I heard a voice just above a whisper. It called me by name. Once, twice, three times. Then it told me to go away and leave it alone.

So I went back downstairs and sat down with my dog. He sat there next to me growling non-stop for two hours. I have been scared ever since.

From 3-6 every day I hear the same noises and my dog still growls. I am now a full believer.

This is a completely and utterly true story. ■

Back From Iraq
Censored, Texas

I am a 21 year old female and live in a small town in Texas. My fiancé was in the Army and had been for three years. He was on his last tour in Iraq and every chance he had he would call.

One day he called and said he couldn't talk long but wanted to tell me he loved me and always would. Not three hours later I got the heartbreaking call. He had been killed in a mission yesterday, his friend told me. I wondered how this could be when I talked to him just a few hours ago.

For the next couple of months I stayed at home miserable and when I finally decided to get out of the house while driving in my car the radio turned off in the middle of one of my favorite songs which he would always do just to irritate me, only this time it just relieved me it made me realize even though I couldn't see him he was still with me.

jIt still happens to this day, almost two years later, and every time it brings a smile to my face. And if I change the background on my phone it somehow always changes back to a picture of me and him. I just laugh and tell him he is stubborn.

As for the call I know it happened no matter who believes me. I know he was calling to say his last goodbye and to make sure I knew he loved me.

The Girl In Red
Bridgeport, Texas

It was my friend Kelsie's birthday. We were all sitting, laughing and messing around.

All of the sudden we heard this high pitch scream coming from the forest from our left. At first we thought it was her family messing with us because her dad loves to play jokes on us so we ignored it.

After an hour, my friend Duiwn got up super fast and ran to the house screaming! We chased after him and asked him what was wrong. He told us that he was drinking his Dr. Pepper and he heard this girl say his name. (I don't know how to even say his name so I call him dippy) So we looked at each other and laughed at him.

We decided to stay inside because the mosquitoes were biting badly. So, we started playing hide and seek and I felt someone push me in the back. I turned around and saw this girl in red run around the corner of the living room to the basement. It then dawned on me that no one was wearing red. Being curious, I followed her. As I came around the corner Kelsie was opening the basement door.

I asked her if she saw a girl in red. With a puzzled face, she said no and ran down the stairs, I followed. As we got to the bottom, we both heard a small bang behind us. We turned around and saw a shadow go to our right to the back corner of the basement behind the junk she has down there.

As we went over to look to see if it was one of our friends; we saw her. She was crouched down looking at us. The girl in red said, "Shh, we have to hide." Then she vanished. We both ran out screaming our butts off!

To this day we still don't know who she is, but it was scary!

Death Walk
Monahans, Texas

This sighting happened one afternoon during the summer of 1980 when I was ten years old. I was alone at home working on my bicycle in the garage. My Dad would be home from work any minute so he was the next person I expected to see.

I caught a movement in the corner of my eye as I was looking down at the broken chain on my bike, and I immediately looked up. It was my Dad walking past the entrance to the garage. He was wearing his usual work attire consisting of blue jeans and a western-style shirt.

I greeted him excitedly with, "Hi, Dad!"

To my surprise and bewilderment, he did not respond. In fact, the expression on his face was blank, as if he were completely oblivious to anything going on around him.

His expression was utterly and completely drained of any sign of awareness of what was going on. He looked straight ahead and continued walking.

I was five feet from him and had no doubt that he heard me, so I was very puzzled at his lack of reaction. I stepped out of the garage to follow him. As soon as I stepped out of the garage he vanished.

Confused more than ever, I began frantically searching for him (as if there were somewhere to hide--which there wasn't). I was in denial and shock that something like this could really happen. While I stood there in bewilderment, my Dad arrived in his truck and I asked him if he had just been there. He could see I was upset and he told me that he had not been there and that, since the person vanished in front of me, it must have been a ghost.

The next summer I found a hammer buried in the dirt a few feet from where the ghost disappeared. The name carved on the wooden handle of the hammer was 'PAW'. I asked my Dad who P.A.W. was, thinking these were initials for someone's name. My Dad then told me about my great-grandfather that everyone called Paw. Dad said the hammer must have belonged to him and must be very old because Paw died back in the 50's.

Paw was quite deaf and sometimes very confused in his old age. He was killed tragically one afternoon while walking into town. He was hit from behind by a train on the tracks that run across the end of our property... directly in line with where I saw the ghost heading.

Something in the House
Seadrift, Texas

I grew up in a two-story Victorian-style home. The house is roughly 150 years old and ever since I can remember there have been weird things happening in the house.

This is my brother's story of his first-hand experience with the "thing" in his room. My brother is one year older than me, and was diagnosed with autism as a kid.

This happened around four years ago. My mom and dad separated and my dad kept the house. My brother, on occasion, would stay at his house. One night my brother had stayed up pretty late (around 2:00-ish), messing with his computer. He normally stays up this late. When he was getting ready for bed and laid down he heard what sounded like breathing, around the area where the closet is.

I need to add in here that the house was in major need of remodeling. The closet in my brother's room had a huge hole in the sheet rock and it led to an unfinished bathroom. Everything collected dust and spider webs in that bathroom, and as kids we weren't allowed in there. The floor was rotten in some places. But back to the story.

The breathing scared him. His first reaction was to cover himself with the thin sheet he had on the bed. He described the breathing as "heavy, like someone with a bad cold." He told me that he pulled the blanket hard over his head, thinking that maybe that would somehow protect him. He listened to the breathing move closer to the bed. Then he saw the outline of a tall, thin figure. The closer the thing got to the bed, the faster and louder the breathing became.

My brother was terrified, he held on to the sheet for dear life. That must have alerted the thing because within a second a long, bony hand became more visible to my brother. He said it happened in slow motion, like how you can watch an accident and it seems like eternity. He describe these abnormally long, bony fingers reach for his head! The thing was trying to reach under the sheet to get his head! The hand was jerking wildly trying to get underneath the thin sheet.

My brother was trying frantically to guard himself, while sobbing! He didn't want to die. With all is might he tried, but it wasn't enough. It got its hand underneath! He passed out right when the thing reached the back of his neck! He told me about it, along with the rest of my family the next day. He says he didn't know what happened after that.

Unfortunately, for months after that he wasn't able to sleep at night. He slept during the day and stayed awake all night. It even got to the point where he slept in the car. My brother was 21 or 22 when that happened. He has never been the type to get scared over every little noise. Something happened to him that night and all of us (my entire family) are afraid of it. Sorry for the long story, I just want to know if anyone else has experienced something like that. ∎

Don't Let It Get You
La Port, Texas

Well this story happened to me when I was visiting my grandma and family in Robstown, Texas which is on the out skirts of Corpus.

So here is my story. We were having a BBQ and I was asked to go down the street to my aunt's house to get the paper plates and silver wear and stuff. All I had to walk is down the street, and four houses later I'm at my aunts.

I unlocked the door and proceeded inside her home and as I was in the kitchen I heard the front door slam and lock. I froze where I stood and then I heard the ugliest growl and gurgling voice say, "Don't bother running 'cause I'm hungry and you're gonna die tonight."

After I heard that I wanted to scream and cry and run out the house but what ever it was, was in the living room so I ran straight to my aunt's room and hid on top of her bed under the covers.

Please don't judge, I was freaking out hard and at the time it sounded like a good idea. The blanket on her bed was huge and fluffy and would allow me to hide well.

As I hid on the bed I heard the door to her room open slowly and could hear something or someone walking around the room and then it left.

I knew I had to make a run for it. I got out of bed slowly and as quiet as I could, but the thing heard me and I could hear it running back towards the room I was in.

I had no other choice so I ran into her small closet and hid there. As I sat on the floor holding the door knob for dear life I could see it entering the room. I kept saying, "Please leave, please leave, please leave," but of course it stopped in front of the closet door. My heart was pounding and I thought I was going to loose it. It grabbed the door and I played tug of war for my life but I guess it thought the door was locked cause it stopped and ran out of the room.

So as I sat there I was thinking, "Why hasn't anyone come to find me?" It doesn't take very long to get the stuff for the BBQ. I decided I couldn't wait any longer because what if they come and it's too late and I'm already dead? All kinds of crazy stuff was going through my head, and I just snapped and decided to make a run for it. If it got me, I'd fight, and if I died, at least I died fighting.

So I said forget it and dashed out of the closet, ran out of the room and through the kitchen. I could see the door and I could hear little footsteps chasing after me not like an adult's footsteps but more like a child and I really wanted to turn my head around to see what it was that was chasing me but I knew I had to get out. I pushed against the front door, unlocked it and ran out! I could feel the tears starting to form in my eyes and the excitement of being free and feeling safe overcame me and I thought I was in a safe zone cause I was two houses away from the BBQ. I could see and hear my family and music and people talking. I stopped running and turned and looked at my aunt's house and there on the front porch with the door open wide and the living room lights shining bright I saw as clear as day what wanted to kill me.

It was a small troll looking thing with greasy, dangling long hair and yellow eyes and its face was so ugly and oddly shaped. The most prevalent thing I remembered was its teeth, because it was smiling at me. I saw the top and bottom rows of nasty sharp teeth. Its body was almost deformed looking. As I turned to start running again I heard it say, "You will be back and I'll get you one way or another."

As I stepped into my grandma's home I ran straight up to the room I was staying in. My husband came in shortly after and I broke down crying telling him everything and he said something that shocked me. He said that he had seen it too, but earlier that day. It was staring through the window when we drove by her house when we went to the store, but he didn't think too much of it because he thought it was the sun playing tricks on his eyes. ■

My Dead Son
Austin, Texas

My wife and I had three boys and two girls. My oldest is 16, then two 13 year-olds, one 10, and the youngest 8. We just moved into a new house because our 10 year old was very sick, and he needed to be closer to the hospital.

A month after we moved in our young 10 year old passed away (he had cancer). My family was in tears for months.

A year after he passed, I was walking by all of my kids' rooms to make sure they were asleep. I walked by Brendan's room (he was the son that had passed), and I looked inside, pretending he was still in there sleeping. A light turned on and I heard Brendan calling for me. All he said was, "Daddy, where are you?" Not believing this, I assumed it was my 8 year old calling me from down the hall, so I walked over but he was fast asleep.

"Strange," I whispered to myself and walked past Brendan's room, but the light was off. I took it as my mind playing tricks on me and went to bed.

Next week, same day, same time, I was walking up the stairs when I saw Brendan standing there with his arms out as if he wanted a hug. I cried and said, "Come here, give Dad a hug." He didn't move. I put my arms down and walked up to where he was, but by the time I got there he disappeared.

I told my wife and she told me that I was still upset and didn't want to accept that Brendan was gone.

I fell asleep, and that night my bedroom door opened and I heard footsteps coming down into my room. I sat up but nothing was there.

Two years went by from this happening, so I finally convinced my wife that we should move because this house had too many bad memories.

So we all got packed up and we put all the boxes in the moving truck. My family took the car so we didn't have to sit in a moving truck, and as I looked outside the car window to say goodbye to our house, I saw Brendan in the window, hands on the glass, and he had tears rolling down his cheeks.

I blew a kiss and we drove away. ∎

Volume 3: Ghost Stories from Texas

Look for more volumes of True Ghost Stories from Joe Kwon

**The End of Volume 3
Joe Kwon's True Ghost Stories
Ghost Stories from Texas**

Have you seen a ghost?

Submit your encounters at

http://www.kwonapps.com/publishing/haunted/

Joe Kwon, Inc.

Joe Kwon's True Ghost Stories. Copyright © 2010, 2011 by Joe Kwon, Inc. All rights reserved. Published and distributed worldwide from the United States of America. No part of this book may be used or reproduced in any manner whatsoever without written permission except in the case of brief quotations embodied in critical articles or reviews. For information, address Joe Kwon, Inc, 3 North Lafayette, Marshall, Missouri 65340.

ISBN-10 0-9828659-2-9, ISBN-13 9780982865927